WAGON TRAIL TO NOWHERE

Wagon Trail to Nowhere

Laurel Means

North Star Press of St. Cloud, Inc.
St. Cloud, Minnesota

Copyright © 2010 Laurel Means

ISBN: 0-87839-388-9
ISBN-13: 978-0-87839-388-6

All rights reserved.

First Edition, July 2010

Printed in the United States of America

Published by
North Star Press of St. Cloud, Inc.
P.O. Box 451
St. Cloud, Minnesota 56302

www.northstarpress.com

FOR

Adrian, Eric, Inigo, and Julia

who followed this trail with me

Table of Contents

Chapter One	One Last Look	1
Chapter Two	On the Trail	22
Chapter Three	The Crossing	35
Chapter Four	A Daring Plan	52
Chapter Five	Among the Buffalo	72
Chapter Six	Dangerous Ways	90
Chapter Seven	Song of the Wolves	112
Chapter Eight	The Haunted Cave	124
Chapter Nine	Disaster Strikes	141
Chapter Ten	Fragments of Hope	159
Chapter Eleven	Choices	178

Chapter 1

ONE LAST LOOK

"WELL, well, Miss, heard anything from your Pa yet?"

Sarah Pearl looked down at her feet, as the fat, red-faced general store proprietor, Mr. Bergstrom, poured the last measure of kerosene into her oil can. "No, sir, I haven't. Are you sure no letters have come for me?"

"Not today, Miss. Know you're disappointed. Your Pa, now, that Will Lundgren—he sure did take off in a strange way. How long's it been, then?"

"Twenty-five days." She'd counted them. Counted them off every day. Each one another day of watching the road down below her homestead cabin. Each night another night of lighting the oil lamp in the parlor window so Papa could see his way home. That was why she'd run out of oil and had to come into Four Corners for more, spending the last twenty-five cents out of Mama's old sugar jar—money kept only for emergencies.

For sure this was an emergency. Why hadn't anyone been able to tell her the truth about why her father had left so suddenly on their horse, Storm—without a word? Without even a note? Nobody in the whole village of Four Corners could tell her anything. No news had come from anywhere else.

"Managing by yourself, are you? Know it ain't easy." Mr. Bergstrom turned off the spigot on the big kerosene tank he kept at the back of the store and replaced the cap on her oil can. "There you go, Miss. I 'spect that'll do you for a while. No, not easy for you, your Pa missing and all."

Sarah Pearl tried to put down a flash of anger at Mr. Bergstrom's words. She knew he meant only to be kind, but they hurt, all the same. They were fast turning hurt into anger. She clenched her hands until her fingers tingled with pain and her breathing came in short gasps. How had Papa expected her to manage by herself?

Indeed, she thought, how had Papa expected her to manage? She was at her wit's end, exhausted, and discouraged. There was only so much she could do, getting up at dawn, hoeing, mucking out the barn, weeding, milking. By the time evening closed the day, she was nearly too tired to eat. Not that there was much left to eat. A few carrots from the garden, a cabbage for soup. She didn't have the heart to kill off any more of the chickens. She needed them for eggs. She didn't dare ask Mr. Bergstrom for more credit beyond the few eggs he bought from her now and then.

"That'll be a quarter, then," Mr. Bergstrom broke into her thoughts. "Anything else I can get for you?" He looked a little embarrassed as he added quietly, "You can put it on credit if you—" There was some reluctance in his tone. She knew she had little or no credit left.

"No, thank you, Mr. Bergstrom. This'll be all." And she slid the quarter across the counter to him, then headed stiffly out the store's front door, trying to keep her head held high as Mrs. Petty and that gossipy old woman, Miss Simonsen, stared at her. Then they exchanged some whispered comments, shaking their heads. She sure wouldn't ask them for help, no matter how desperate it got.

"You're sure, now, Miss Lundgren," Mr. Bergstrom called after her, following her out to the boardwalk along the front of his store, "sure there's nothing else?"

"No—thank you," she managed to say without turning her head.

Heading east toward home, she could hardly think straight. That man had so unsettled her. And then those two old women. It was bad enough that Mrs. Simonsen reminded her of her Aunt Margaret. She'd been so fond of Aunt Margaret. What a pity that she and Uncle Jack had left Four Corners a year ago. Headed west with a wagon train, expecting a homestead out in Montana. More opportunities out there, they'd insisted.

If only she knew where Aunt Margaret and Uncle Jack were now. She could write them a letter and ask for money. She was sure they'd send it right away. But searching through Papa's desk after he'd disappeared revealed no address. Only some bills, some old Christmas cards, and a couple of letters from someplace in Ohio.

The Ziebes' homestead was just ahead. She could hear someone chopping wood behind the barn. With a sharp intake of breath, she resolved to see him and turned off the road at the big oak tree. A well-rutted track let alongside it to the barnyard, then turned into a grassy path leading around the barn to the kitchen garden behind it.

She looked longingly at the rows of beans, loaded with slender green pods. At the high staked tomato plants. There was so little left in her own garden.

Mr. Ziebe looked up in surprise. "Why if it ain't Miss Lundgren. Heard anything from your Pa yet?"

There it was, that same awkward question. "No, sir. Not yet." She set down the oil can, growing heavier by the minute.

"Anything I can do for you?" His words seemed to be at odds with the pained expression on his face and the way he drew back his shoulders. As if he'd done enough already and wasn't eager to do more.

"Wheat harvest coming up end of August."

"Know that," he said slowly, leaning on his axe handle.

"I was wondering, Mr. Ziebe, if you'd be willing to help with that. Give you a couple bales of hay for your trouble. I'm sure my father will pay you something when he comes back."

"You expect him back then? Soon?" There was sarcasm in his question.

"I don't know, I expect so." *I hope so.*

He hesitated. Then, after a long pause, took up his axe and came down with a splitting crash against a section of a thick oak log. "Don't know 'bout that. I'll talk to the Clarks, they might be willin'. Them eighty acres of yours, though—awful big job to look after, even with your Pa around. And that hay along the Red Wing River—mighty hard to scythe, even when the ground's dry."

Sarah Pearl's heart sank. Already, already, she'd asked too much of her neighbors. Once again that feeling of helplessness overwhelmed her. "I'd sure appreciate it, Mr. Ziebe," was all she could manage as she turned back down the grassy path toward the main road.

It was a long hot, dusty walk back to the cabin, a good mile farther down the Goshen Road. Each footstep sent up a cloud of golden dust. Each footstep closer to home meant sooner having to face an empty house, those chores awaiting her. By the time she arrived home, she was hot and thirsty. It was almost too much to bear, after all that, when she discovered the water bucket was empty. But she was too tired to go down to the spring by the river to fill it.

Instead, she set the oil can down on the kitchen floor by the table as she fell into the old rocking chair, her Pa's favorite chair. Burying her face in her hands, she felt dry sobs pulsing against her whole frame. Yes, it was too much. She couldn't go on much longer like this. She felt her eyes closing, her body sinking in more heavily into the arms of the chair.

"Are you Sarah Pearl Lundgren?"

Sarah Pearl's head jerked up. At first she saw nothing except a tall, dark figure silhouetted in the front doorway with the light behind her. This was strange—hadn't she shut the door behind her and locked it as she always did?

"Well, I aass-ssume you are William Lundgren's-ss daughter?" The voice was odd—high pitched, crackling, a hiss between words. Snake-like. It made Sarah Pearl shiver.

Squinting her eyes against the light, she now made out a woman dressed in a black dress and wearing a heavy black bonnet, the kind widows wore, with a long veil hiding her face in dark shadow. Her repeated words seemed to come out of the dark hollow of her veiled bonnet. *Tap—tap—tap.* Her cane tapped impatiently on the floorboards.

"I—well I don't—" Sarah Pearl drew back instinctively. There was something about this woman . . .

"Cat got your tongue, then? Don't need an anss-sswer, know perfectly well who you are. Proprietor down at the general store told me where I could find you. Don't know me, eh? I'm miss-ssus Kerber, widow Kerber, a diss-ant relative of your Pa's."

The name sounded vaguely familiar. Not long ago, probably a couple of months ago—well before he'd disappeared— Papa had brought a letter back from Bergstroms'. That evening he sat at the kitchen table, reading and re-reading it by the light of the oil lamp.

Who's the letter from? she'd asked him.

He looked thoughtful. Oh, a distant relative, back in Ohio. Hardly remember them. It was years back. As I recall, we were second or third cousins or something like that.

That was all Papa said, but he seemed very moody, even distant after that. Every once in a while he'd take that letter out and read it again. Kerber, she heard him mutter, yes, that family over in Morristown. Remember them, but it's been a long time. Then he'd never said another word about them, or the letter. As if he had something else on his mind, something really bothering him.

And now here was this strange woman named Kerber. She must be connected to that letter, somehow. Her sudden appearance in the doorway was scary, her looks even more so.

"Cat got your tongue, eh," the woman repeated. "I understand your father's gone? Just up and left? How long's it been, then? Never mind . . . got all that from Bergstrom."

She waved the end of her cane around the room, pointing at first one object, then another. "Place here not in good shape, I ss-see. Wouldn't expect a young girl like you to manage on your own."

Sarah Pearl's alarm was turned quickly into anger. "But I've been managing, thank you."

"The crops? The ss-stock? Don't look like it to me, from what I ss-saw coming. Weeds-ss a mile high, milk cow looking poorly, calf thin as a rail. And just look at this place." She pointed her cane around the parlor. "Dust. Cobwebs. Dirty dishes on the floor. What have you been doing? Better yet, what do you intend to do?"

"Why, stay here of course. Wait for Papa."

"What if he ain't never coming back, eh?"

The idea was a shock. Never coming back? The thought hadn't occurred to her.

"Real possibility, ain't it?"

What if it was? What could she do? The feeling of helplessness came over her like a dark fog, a stifling fog that seemed to choke the life out of her. Had the fact that she'd used up the last of the lamp oil been a sign? A portend of doom? Never coming back . . . ?

"Now ss-see here," the woman insisted, sitting herself down decisively on the old horsehair sofa by the parlor window but continuing to tap her cane on the floorboards. "Ss-some time ago, Mr. Kerber, my husband, may the Lord rest his soul, wrote to your Pa. Told him we were planning to move out west, joining the Johnson wagon train from Ohio. Homesteads-ss out there, place in Montana."

So that was what that letter was all about, Sarah Pearl was thinking. That place called Montana—something familiar about the name. "Montana?"

"Mr. Kerber thought he'd like to persuade your Pa to join us."

Sarah Pearl caught her breath—what was left of it after that dark fog had sucked most of it out of her body. "Go out there?"

"Yes-s. More land, bigger spread than this-ss one here, I can ss-see. And from the looks of it, you're not doing too well. Won't be much harvest come September, I reckon. I noticed coming along the road that something's got into your wheat."

"Go out there? Papa was going to—"

"Don't reckon I know for ss—sure. We got delayed crossing the Missis-ss-sippi. Mr. Kerber, Lord rest his ss-soul, took poorly. We had to stay for a spell, expecting him to get better.

Wagon train had to go on ahead. After he pass-ssed away, well then, we came on. Intended to stop by to see your pa. Now I find he ain't here. Only you."

"I—I—" was all she managed to say.

"Only you, and on your own, for land's sake. What do you intend to do?"

"I—I—" Sarah Pearl repeated. After a few seconds, she drew up her shoulders and stiffened her back. She wasn't quite sure with what kind of resolve, but she had to stand up to this woman somehow. She'd developed an instinctive dislike for her. She wasn't sure why.

Perhaps it had something to do with the fact that this woman, this Kerber family, had intended to persuade them to leave their homestead in Four Corners, the only home she'd ever known, the place near where Mama and her little brother Jason were buried in Lakeview Cemetery. She could not believe that her father would ever be willing to leave this cabin, this farm, for which he'd work so hard all these years. And he was going to return here. How could he do otherwise? "I'll manage, ma'am. I've been managing just fine."

The Kerber woman snorted, tapping her cane even more impatiently against the floor. "Not likely. Not likely, by the looks of things." She paused to take another look around the room, poked at the dirty dishes on the floor with her cane. There was another snort. "Best pack up your things-ss. Can't leave you here alone, just a young girl. No telling what might happen. Your father would want you to come with us—only kin I know of you've got. "

She got to her feet so suddenly that the sofa springs gave several raspy squeaks. "So, young Miss, you're coming with us-ss. Day after tomorrow. Wagon'll be ready then. We can't wait any longer. The Johnson wagon train'll already be getting too far ahead of us."

"But what if Papa—"

For a moment the woman looked thoughtful and turned to stare out the front parlor window. "That will be as will be. Mr. Kerber was sure your pa intended to sell this place and come with us."

"Papa never told me that."

"More's the pity."

"It's hard to believe. I always thought—"

"Well, Miss, whatever you may or may not believe, I insist that you come along with us-ss. It's-ss the best solution to your ss-situation."

"What if he comes back *soon*?" She hoped so much that would be the case. She dreamed of it at night, day-dreamed during the day. Over and over again she visualized that wonderful, ecstatic moment when she heard Storm come clip-clopping into the barnyard carrying Papa, the sound of his light step on the back stoop, and his tall, broad-shoulders framed in the kitchen doorway.

"What if he comes back?" She shook her head, looking skeptical. "Gone so long—don't seem—" she stopped, obviously reluctant to express her doubts. She added, in a somewhat softer tone it seemed to Sarah Pearl, "I'll instruct Bergstrom at the store to tell your pa that you're with us-ss and what trail the wagon train is-ss takin'. Then when—" here she paused and shook her head slightly, "*if*—if he ever catches up, then you can decide what to do."

"But I—"

"No, there's-ss no room for argument, girl." She pointed her cane directly at Sarah Pearl like a weapon. "Get this place closed up. Get neighbors to look after the stock. You be ready, too, hear? We can't wait any longer, not for a whole host of reasons." The next minute she was gone, as quickly and invisibly as she'd come.

It took Sarah Pearl a few minutes to collect herself after this unnerving encounter. It left her with a strange, prickly feeling, something she couldn't really explain. It was as if that woman had cast some kind of spell on her and taken over her mind and will. With a shudder, she closed and bolted hard the door.

For the rest of the day, Sarah Pearl struggled with that feeling, at times rebelling against it and the anger it generated. How dare that woman come in here like that? How dare she tell her what to do? Leave her home? What if Papa came while she was gone—what would he think? How would he find her? There were a whole lot of trails west, she'd heard, and hundreds of wagon trains. It'd be like looking for a needle in a haystack.

But it was no use. She seemed powerless to resist the woman's will, the woman's argument. She had to recognize the truth, and the truth was that she was being overpowered by responsibilities greater than she could manage, and she could not manage much longer. Here was the brutal truth, the reality of the situation. The longer her father was gone, the more run-down the place would become. He'd come back to ruins, yes ruins! It would be all her fault. He'd blame her. Then he'd end up selling the homestead and heading west anyway, probably leaving her once again.

That evening she did not bother to light the oil lamp and place it on the table in the parlor window. Not bothering to undress, she lay all night in her clothes on the parlor sofa, oblivious to the squeaky springs, trying hard to push out of her mind the afternoon's visit with that Mrs. Kerber, who'd been sitting on this very sofa. Her mind spun in a turmoil in between fitful moments of troubled sleep. Horrible images of a witch-like figure danced through her brain, hissing line a snake, pointing a stick at her.

Next morning her yellow gingham dress was damp with sweat and twisted around her legs, trying to bind her and hold her back. It was difficult to stand, and she had to hold onto the sofa arm until she got herself untangled. The air was hot and heavy, draining away what little energy she had left. She had not the strength to brush out her long blonde hair and re-braid it. Her beautiful hair. Papa had been so proud of it. She did not bother to change her clothes, as uncomfortable as they were, strangling her body like tight, clammy bands.

All that morning she picked at the dried-out remains of a loaf of bread she'd baked three days before, not hungry, hardly tasting it. The rest of the day she walked around in a daze. She knew she had much to do. She recognized some truth in the Kerber woman's argument, something that made better sense than she was prepared to accept. Yet to leave now, with the possibility of her father's return—

No, the woman was right. What if not? Not now nor even later? There was no way out but to follow the woman's instructions and head out to Montana in their covered wagon.

Remembering the place—Montana. A sudden connection, an instantaneous flicker of reasoning. Her Aunt Margaret and Uncle Jack had gone there—somewhere. A connection—a hope perhaps of finding them.

But first, the house had to be shut down. Sarah Pearl scarcely knew where to begin. She picked up this item, that item, changed her mind, set it down. She tried to focus her mind on what to do with the livestock, the chickens. She'd have to ask another neighbor, Hans Olson, to see to that. She couldn't ask the Clarks for anything more. Her mind simply wouldn't focus on details. It was as if the Widow Kerber had somehow possessed it.

The next day as if in a daze she spread her still damp yellow gingham dress over a chair back to dry. She had to wear something else. She had no choice but to open the big chest where Papa had always kept her mother's things and take out a clean camisole, petticoat, and long white stockings. They were her mother's and a bit large but fit well enough under the dark blue and yellow calico dress, which she normally used for second-best occasions. She hardly remembered packing a few other things into a carpet bag—a spare petticoat of her mother's, her own best pink silk dress, her mother's heart-shaped locket, an old, faded picture inside. Unthinkingly she pushed back her thick blonde braids and tied her yellow sunbonnet under her chin.

Still in a daze, she walked the two miles down Goshen Road to Bergstrom's store. The trees alongside the road passed slowly by in a green haze. The dust rose under her feet in disregarded dry puffs. She was only aware of the fact that her lungs felt squeezed together and that time seemed not measurable by any familiar units.

Vaguely she noticed passing alongside a big wagon in the stable yard before the store, a prairie schooner with a canvas cover, a team of oxen already hitched to the yoke. A saddle horse was tied behind the wagon, and a small boy in a checked shirt and straw hat seemed to be helping Mr. Bergstrom's hired man, George, load provisions into the wagon. A baby was crying inside the wagon.

What attracted her attention, however, was the fact that the boy looked about the same age her brother Jason would be, had he lived. As she watched him, he clambered up into the wagon, disappeared inside, then climbed down with a baby in his arms. Not exactly a baby, though. It looked more like a two-year old or maybe it was three. "Hush, now, Sophie," the boy kept repeating, as he rocked her back and forth. "Here, I'll walk a bit with you." He stared at Sarah Pearl as he passed, then quickly turned with the child around the other side of the wagon.

Were these the Kerbers? Sarah Pearl wondered. There hadn't been any mention of children. The fact cast a slightly different light on Mrs. Kerber. Witches normally didn't have children—or did they?

"Ah, Miss, there you are," boomed Mr. Bergstrom as Sarah Pearl entered the store. Wiping his hands on his white apron, which scarcely covered his fat belly, he commented, "And just in time, too. We were getting worried. I was about to send George down after you."

"Mail?" she found herself asking shakily, hopefully.

"No, I'm sorry to say. But I'll keep checking. And I must say, Miss, I believe you've made the right decision. I'm sure folks 'round here will agree with me. You'll be far better off, although I wonder about the Kerbers—"

Tap—tap—tap! The Widow Kerber silenced him with a warning tap of her cane on the counter, and he quickly changed the subject.

"Well, ahem, as I was about to say, the Kerbers are almost loaded up and ready to leave. Young Tom's been out there helping George." He bowed a little toward the widow. "Now, ma'am, if you'll excuse me, I'll go back and check off your list. I'll have the reckoning in just a moment."

It seemed to Sarah Pearl that the Widow Kerber fixed her eyes on her for a full minute or two, beady black eyes like a snake, thinking, calculating. It caused that same prickly feeling all down Sarah Pearl's spine. She tried to look away, but found it difficult. She felt beads of sweat break out on her forehead. Fear, anxiety—such confused emotions left her feeling weak in the knees. Leaving—staying—leaving—what was she doing?

Finally the widow said in her strangely unnerving voice, "Ss-ssooo, you are here, I ss-see." She turned toward a tall boy standing behind her, and pushed him forward. "My elder son, Michael. Man of the family now. Fine young man. Nineteen next winter. Your distant cousin."

Her cousin? That person? That woman—her aunt? Horrors! How could that be? How distant? Centuries, she hoped.

The said cousin, Michael Kerber, just smirked and stared at Sarah Pearl like she was some kind of freak. Then he tossed back his head of curly black hair, squinted his eyes to narrow slits, snorted, and turned away. "Got to check on the replacement ox harnesses," he muttered and stalked off.

"Looks like it's all done, ma'am." Mr. Bergstrom returned with a sheet of paper in his hand as he replaced a stubby pencil behind his ear. Lot of provisions needed, you realize, for the five of you. It's quite a long trek. Hmm, let me see, a keg of corn meal, several jugs of molasses, a side of smoked ham, a twenty-pound sack of flour, and—and—" he ran down the list. Then he patted Sarah Pearl on the arm as he said, "I'm sure the Kerbers expect you to offer you help for your keep, Miss. You can do that by being helpful on the journey."

With a terrible shock, his remarks forced Sarah Pearl to realize something for the first time. From the looks of all that stuff going into the wagon, they were expecting her to be helpful to them for a very long time. It wouldn't have been so bad could she consider them as family. No, that would never happen.

"Ready to go, ma'am." George entered the store and handed the Widow Kerber a small basket. "Thought you might like to keep these vittals close by. Everything else stowed proper like."

"All right, then, missus Kerber," said Mr. Bergstrom. I'll just help you up onto the driving bench, then see you off. And may I wish you a good journey?" He coughed slightly. "And a safe one?"

The Widow Kerber gave no acknowledgement, but brushed past him and tapped her way out of the store, across its porch, and waited for Michael to help her up into the wagon. "Hand me the baby, Tom," she said to the boy Sarah Pearl had seen helping George. "I'll take her up here with me 'til that girl knows what she's supposed to do. You and her get in the back. Make sure that tailgate's shut proper. Don't want nothin' fallin' out on the trail."

Sarah Pearl silently followed the widow's clipped instructions, and she and Tom settled in the back of the stuffed wagon. Then Sarah Pearl felt the big oxen slowly strain the wagon into motion. She looked out the back. Mr. Bergstrom was standing on the front steps of his general store in his big straw hat, waving a big white handkerchief and shouting something about having a good journey.

Sitting on the floor at the back of the wagon with young Tom Kerber, Sarah Pearl Lundgren hardly heard him as she looked out through the canvas opening. She tried to take one long, last look down the road behind them, the one leading east back home.

One last look at the store where her father used to buy her a penny's worth of candy when the wheat harvest was good. The store where she'd bought her father's last birthday present, only a few days before he'd disappeared. The store where she'd spent her last bit of money to buy oil for a lamp, which would now not be lit. It was hopeless. Her eyes were too full of tears to see much. Everything was just a blur.

Was she sad or angry? Maybe both. Maybe mostly angry. How could her father just leave like that? She sucked in her breath, suddenly realizing something in a flash of revelation, something she'd tried hard to suppress during the past four weeks. Suppose something had happened to Papa? Suppose he wasn't ever coming back?

Her eyes burned as she fought back tears. *Can't show anybody I care*, Sarah Pearl kept repeating to herself. She squeezed her eyes shut and clenched her fists. *Be brave! Now listen, Pearl, you can do it!*

Yes, it was time to follow her own advice. She straightened up and threw back her shoulders. Won't even look back at that old store. *Old Mr. Bergstrom and his white handkerchief!* So Sarah Pearl deliberately turned her head away as the wagon pulled out of the stable yard. A sudden jolt as the oxen picked up speed made her hang on more tightly to the wagon's tailgate.

Won't look back, Sarah Pearl kept repeating to herself. *Won't! Won't!* The wagon began jolting and swaying from the roughness of the road as it entered the main westward trail. As far as Sarah Pearl was concerned, it was the trail to nowhere.

"Hup—hup!" The voice of Michael Kerber came back from the front of the wagon. The snake-like voice of Mrs. Kerber telling him what to do. As if a boy like that would listen to anybody. Now the baby crying at the top of her lungs.

"Bye-bye, Sarah Pearl! Be sure to—" Fainter and fainter the words from Mr. Bergstrom in the growing distance.

No! She couldn't go on. She had to go back, no matter what. *Stop! Oh stop!* Sarah Pearl wanted to yell to that boy driving the wagon. *You know I can manage by myself*, she wanted to shout to his mother.

But she only choked from the thick dust rising behind the wheels of the wagon. The dust also stung her eyes. Yes, for sure it was only dust. She wasn't about to break down crying. Not in front of any of the Kerbers. Especially that boy, Tom, sitting next to her in the back of the wagon. She knew he'd been put there to guard her from running back home.

Looking at the trail disappearing behind her, it was harder and harder to see anything at all. There was so much dust, not only rising up from the trail but also settling thickly on the brush alongside. Above her were dark stands of overhanging pine branches. Over in the distance the bright silver flash of a lake. But everything around her was becoming more and more unfamiliar. She had never been this far this side of Four Corners and already felt lost.

How far had they come? How far back the store? Whatever Papa had done, wherever he was—she'd forgive him. Yes, she would. She would! And she needed to be home whenever —if ever—he came back

If . . . if . . . if . . . Her mind whirled around and around. What should she do? What was it she really wanted? Now so confused, she scarcely felt the sharp jolts where the big wagon wheels bounced over rocks or fell into deep ruts. No, she felt numb. She knew only that she'd lost something important. That she was now alone. She was in a kind of daze, a kind of spell, with little will of her own.

"Watch out, Miss. You're 'bout to fall out over the wagon tailgate!" Tom grabbed her arm. "Maw said to keep an eye on you. She's got to stay up there with Sophie and help Michael drive."

"Help him drive?"

"It's really Michael who's driving, you know. Thinks he's the man of the family now. But sometimes he needs a little help with the team. He won't admit it. Ha! Betcha I could do better! Old Big Horn and Blue—them oxen, they listen to me, you know, 'cause I learned ox talk."

An eye on her. Ox talk. How silly! She was beginning to dislike all of them, and it had started with the Widow Kerber. But this Tom now, with his curly black hair, like his brother. Why'd he have to remind her of so much of Jason? Just to look at him brought back painful memories of her little brother.

Jason—drowned two years ago. Why'd he have to wander off like that in the first place? She could have saved him, if only she'd done like Mama had told her, not to let him go down into the pasture along the Red Wing River. If only she hadn't been thinking about the new dress Papa had promised her, about Mama being so sick and all. If only—if only . . . All those ifs again . . .

"And if you don't watch out, Miss," continued Tom, squeezing her arm so hard it hurt, "you'll fall out of the wagon next time we hit a big hole." He sighed. "Guess I could grab them long braids down your back. That'd sure pull you back!"

"Don't you dare touch my hair." Sarah Pearl was proud of her long hair, which curled at the ends where the braids ended. Even if it was hard to keep the little wisps around her face tucked in. Papa called them spit-curls.

Tom continued, a jeering look on his face. "Ain't you got no sense? Why'd you have to come along with us, anyways? One more mouth to feed. Hard enough as it is." Tom looked like he was about to push her out onto the trail. "Sure's anything, Michael won't care one little bit if you fell out. Huh! Wouldn't stop for you, neither! Him and me, well, we'd just as soon leave you lying down there in the dust."

Well, wasn't that just what she wanted? Out of that wagon? But what had he said? Michael won't care. Not surprising—she didn't care for him, either. He'd been so rude in the store.

Even worse, he looked a little like Jason, too. Maybe his black hair was a little longer, his eyes different—not Jason's clear blue like her own, but cold, steely slits. Brrrr—made you shiver. Was he some kind of witch like his mother? She'd heard that men could be witches, too. They were called . . . warlocks.

Tom grabbed her arm again. It hurt more this time, and she shoved him away. "Let go! I'm not going to fall out of the wagon, if that's what you think." *But I may just decide to jump out*, she thought to herself. *As soon as I see a chance*.

"Can't say as your falling out of this wagon would be a great loss, Miss," Tom answered, rolling up his eyes. "Maw wouldn't be too pleased about that, though. Thinks you'll help with the baby and all. Bet you don't know much about babies, or trekking either."

"You might be surprised," she retorted. "What do you know, anyway?"

"Naw, you got a lot to learn—heard Michael carrying on with Maw about that. Us, you know—we been trekking since Ohio. Must've been about two months now—sure do lose track of time, though."

"Well, for your information, Mister Tom, I know a lot more'n you think! So there!"

"About trekking out West? Naw, you're too used to an easy life. You'll be just useless. I know it, Michael knows it, and Maw'll soon find out!" With that, Tom leaped over the tailgate and ran along behind the wagon for a moment. "Got to get me some fresh air, think I'll ride alongside on Boone for a spell. Named him for old Daniel Boone, you see. He gets mighty restless being tied behind us most of the time. But gotta talk to Michael, first."

He kicked up his heels and disappeared around the side of the wagon, easily running faster than the plodding oxen. Sarah Pearl heard him climb up onto the driving bench and complain to Michael and his mother. She knew it was about her. Bad words, for sure.

If only Mama were still alive. If only this awful cramped wagon, that screaming baby, these awful, rude and insensitive boys, that strange woman—if they weren't tearing her away from her own home, from her memories of Mama and Jason.

Sarah Pearl tried hard to bring up happy thoughts. Maybe the best was five years ago—maybe it was 1865, she wasn't quite sure, that Papa came home from the war—that terrible war between the North and the South. That day a stranger's wagon pulled up to the front door of the cabin, and Papa climbed out. Even Mama couldn't think of what to say for a whole two minutes.

It was too bad his wound never healed well. Mama worried so much about it, but it seemed like she couldn't do anything. Yet strangely, it was Mama took so sick, and Papa didn't seem to be able to do anything about that.

And now Sarah Pearl was in this awful, jolting wagon, bumping down a dusty trail, to who knew where. Forced to come. Her own kind of war. She was in pain—not in her leg like Papa, but in her head and her heart. And a prisoner. She had to have a last look, to see if he might suddenly be standing there talking to Mr.Bergstrom. He'd be asking him where she'd gone, and Mr. Bergstrom would tell him. Any minute he'd be galloping after her on Storm. She shaded her eyes and looked back, squinting against the dust to catch the first sight of Storm, with Papa on him.

But she was for a moment distracted by the sounds of that witch, Mrs. Kerber, talking to Michael up front above the baby's crying. And the wagon wheels creaking, banging as they went over rocks, then the wind overhead whipping branches this way and that.

But now, out of all those sounds, Sarah Pearl distinctly heard her own name. Puur—ul! See—eek—Puurr—uul . . . come . . . Pearl! Papa's pet name for her! Who else knew it besides Papa?

Chapter 2

ON THE TRAIL

AT the sound of her name, and with all her strength, Sarah Pearl threw herself over the wagon tailgate. "Ow—uhh!" She landed smack on her backside in the middle of the trail. "Ow—oh! My arm, my arm." She sputtered and coughed from dust choking her throat. Then she realized, *no noise!* They would know something was wrong.

Slowly and painfully she rolled over to the side of the trail into some bushes. Had the wagon stopped? She knew her heart had stopped, just hoping they hadn't noticed anything.

Listening carefully, expecting the worse, she heard the rumble of wagon wheels growing fainter and fainter. Good! They suspected nothing! Wincing from the pain in her arm, she got to her feet and looked down the trail. The wagon had rounded a bend. The trail was empty. She started running in the opposite direction, back toward Bergstrom's store, back toward home. "Ow!" She tripped over a rock, then snagged her foot in a stray tree root.

A few more minutes of running, stumbling, gasping for breath, any minute expecting to hear the Kerbers' wagon coming back to stop her, she saw the building behind some trees just ahead of her.

She stopped dead in her tracks. "That building I thought was Bergstrom's—only an old barn," she said, disappointment making her head swim, her knees buckling under her. "Store's too far back there. Too late, can't make it."

But now the wagon was way ahead in the opposite direction. No sound of it. A deadly silence everywhere. She sat down on an old log beside the trail and buried her face in her hands. She was shaking, but tears refused to come.

"What'll I do now?" she gasped. "Can't go back—those Kerbers already are too far ahead. It'll be dark in a few hours." She'd never felt so helpless, so alone before, not even when her mother died, for then she'd still had her father. But now there was no one, no one—

Clip clop, clip clop. A horse coming, but from which direction? Her heart beat very fast. The joy of hope! Papa coming after her! He'd returned and come to take her home. "Papa! Papa!" she yelled, jumping up in wild expectation and waving her arms. "Papa! Here I am!" *Clip clop, clip clop.* A terrified moment of fear. What if it wasn't Papa? What if it was a stranger? Could she trust him?

She backed off the trail into a thicket of cedars, hoping she couldn't be seen from the road. The horse was coming closer and closer, its hooves striking the hardened ruts, its harness jingling. Then it stopped. Through the branches, she could see the horse's legs—three white and one brown. They looked familiar.

"Whoa, then, Boone! Steady, boy. All right, Miss, you can come out now. Hurt yourself? Told you so. Serves you right, too, falling out of the wagon like that!" The horse moved closer. "Come on, Miss, I can see your old yeller sunbonnet from here. Get out of them cedars. We gotta hurry back 'fore Michael gets any farther ahead." Tom charged Boone partway into the cedars. "Told you you'd fall out if you kept on like that."

Sarah Pearl was torn, disappointed the rider wasn't Papa, or even Mr. Bergstrom—only Tom. Yet she was relieved, though she hated to admit it. Even though the rescue, if she could call it that, meant going back to the wagon among those strangers, each mile farther from home, each moment distancing her from that moment when her father would set his food on the kitchen doorstep.

"Come on then. Best get up here on old Boone, or we'll be stuck out here in the middle of nowhere. Dark soon. Bears out here, too. Grrrrr!" He imitated a growl as he turned the horse around. "Maybe you can get up behind me from that log over there."

Sarah Pearl hesitated. Which was worse—Tom or the bears? She pulled herself up behind Tom by hanging on to his belt and then, hiking up her long skirt, slid her right leg over the horse's flank.

"Better hang on, Miss. I can make this old horse fly like the wind!"

It took all her strength to hang on to Tom. Several times she was sure she'd fall off. After what seemed ages, they came over the top of a hill to see the rear of the wagon moving slowly about fifty yards ahead.

"Michael, Michael!" Tom began to yell. "Slow down, will ya? Got her, whatever you think 'bout that!" Coming alongside the wagon," Tom said. "Best get inside, Miss. Can't stop. Got to make good time now 'fore sunset. See, all 'cause a you, sun going down already."

And so Sarah Pearl felt herself falling back over the wagon's tailgate, exhausted, her arm hurting, her throat dry and choking, eyes burning, her expectations crushed. It seemed so final. An end to hope, and she was trapped and helpless. She lay down on the cramped floor between the boxes and a big chest, under the clothes and tools and bags swaying from pegs on the wagon posts, and moaned into her sunbonnet ties, bunching them up close to her face to muffle the sound.

The ride seemed rougher. It tortured her aching body, but the semi-darkness provided some relief. Against the canvas cover over the wagon's hoops, shadowy patterns made by tree branches under which they passed provided a temporary distraction. But that distraction lasted for only a few moments. She had another pattern in her brain, one which would not go away.

Mr. Bergstrom's words kept oozing back into her mind, however much she fought against it. *You'll be a great help . . . better off with a family who can care for you . . . once they reach their homestead in the Dakotas—Montana—Dakotas—Montana—*

Well, was it Montana? Would she be able to find her aunt and uncle? They were big territories, she'd heard. But surely her father would come after her first. Mr. Bergstrom would tell him about the Kerbers, and Papa would find a way to track them. Any day now, she was sure to see him coming up behind the wagon, waving his old army hat—which he kept, saying it was still useful. He'd be calling her name, "Pearl—Puurll!"

Unfortunately, this happy fantasy dissolved into a more realistic image generated by the facts. He had simply disappeared. What had happened? Four Corners was only a village, where usually everybody knew everything. Before he disappeared, her father hadn't said anything or taken anything like clothes or food. She'd just assumed he was going into Green Prairie for provisions or something, or perhaps the blacksmith for shoeing Storm. He'd mentioned something about that earlier.

But night came. Then the next day. And the next. No word. She asked and asked. And now with every mile this jolting, cramped, rough wagon traveled, she was farther away from finding out the truth. The truth those Kerbers were preventing her from knowing. She was sure she would only find out by returning home. If he still hadn't returned, she'd go in search of him, exactly how she wasn't sure. She would find a way.

With her body drained by her frustrated attempt to leave the wagon and her brain exhausted by such a multitude of thoughts, anxieties, and hopes, she finally fell asleep on the hard, jolting, wagon floor. It was a troubled sleep but a deep one. She was unaware of anything until she woke up the next morning, still curled up in a corner of the wagon. Someone had put a quilt around her during the night. Outside she heard the sounds of camp being struck, cooking utensils being scraped clean, put away, oxen being set into the wagon yoke. That boy Michael ordering people around. Sophie yelling about something.

Now Tom was looking in through the wagon's back flap. "Gonna sleep all day? Ain't you gonna be any help 'round here? Should've left you back there at Four Corners—or with them bears!" With that he spat into some bushes and disappeared.

"Hup! Hup! Haw!" With a command from Michael on the driving bench and a sharp jolt, the wagon creaked forward, throwing Sarah Pearl against some piled boxes. They were once more heading toward where she did not—ever, in a thousand years—want to go.

A week and seemingly endless miles passed. Becoming part of the Kerber family was proving as impossible as she'd expected. They didn't belong to her, she didn't belong to them. They didn't even seem to want her with them.

And wasn't it bad enough that they weren't part of a large wagon train? In a single covered wagon crossing the plains, they were in constant danger, without companionship, without protection.

That Michael—what could he do? Older than she was, but not as smart, she was sure. Yesterday he tried to shoot a rabbit for supper. He missed. They ate only beans and that disgusting salt pork from the barrel. So salty. She lay awake most of the night, dying of thirst. It would have been nice to be part of a group, but, no, there was no one else. Only the Kerbers, day after day. Only Michael, Tom, baby Sophie—oh, and Mrs. Kerber. Her strangeness, her distance, her lack of what Sarah Pearl considered normal emotions, were troubling.

"What's the matter with your Maw," she finally got up enough nerve to ask Tom in the middle of the third week on the trail. She didn't dare ask Michael.

"What d'ya mean?" he answered indignantly.

"I mean why does she talk so funny? Like a snake."

"Talk funny? What do you mean. Talks like Maw, like she's always done. Like everybody else. Matter of fact, you talk kinda funny yourself. Like you was stuck up or something."

Sarah Pearl ignored that remark. "No, I mean she hisses. Hiss—ssss—ssses."

"Oh, that. Heard Paw once say to somebody, Mr. Johnson maybe, something to do with her tongue. Born that way, Paw said. Paw, though, he kinda liked it. Thought is sounded kinda—well, can't remember the word." He paused, looking troubled. "Sure do miss Paw. Taught me how to ride. Yup, miss him." And with that Tom immediately ran off to fetch water from a nearby watering hole, shouting something about how he hoped it wasn't poisonous, like the last one.

Painful thoughts—maybe other people could have them, too. Yet they could never be as painful as her own. No, that was impossible.

A few more days passed without any sign of the Johnson wagon train ahead, even though, with the flat, endless expanse of the grasslands, hardly a tree in sight, they could see miles ahead. Nor was there any sign of a rider following them, her father coming after her to bring her home. The leaden weight in Sarah Pearl's heart grew heavier just as her relations with the Kerbers seemed to grow worse.

"What's the matter with you, Miss? Don't you know anything?" Michael said rudely one morning as she stirred cornmeal, baking soda, and water in the heavy iron skillet over the campfire in order to made breakfast johnnycake. "Can't even keep a fire going with them buffalo cakes?"

"But they're so disgusting," she answered.

"To you, maybe. Not much wood out here on the prairie—got to use what we can find. And that dried buffalo poop's as good as anything."

He grabbed the hot skillet handle with the corner of his jacket and slid it over to the middle of the portable grate, then poked a couple of buffalo cakes into the fire with a stick until they caught. "Besides," he added as he hurried off to hitch up the ox team, "your johnnycake ain't nearly as good as Maw's. What a waste of cornmeal! Aggh, don't know as I'll even try it! Not that hungry!" He pretended to gag. "Worse'n finding weevils in it!"

At that moment Mrs. Kerber, carrying baby Sophie in one arm, with the other digging in her cane step by step, came around the corner of the wagon. She set the toddler down on the grass and said brusquely, "Here, girl, look after her. I've got other thingss-sss to do. And wash these thingss-ss up, as I've got to help Michael see to the oxen."

"Soooo," Sarah Pearl whispered to Sophie as soon as Mrs. Kerber was out of earshot, "your big old brother isn't all he thinks he is. Did you hear that? Your mother needs to help him." She suppressed a dry kind of laugh. "And as for this johnny cake—your big, wonderful brother made the fire too hot and turned it into charcoal. Could have told him so. But he doesn't have feelings, does he? He's like your weird mother. But we care, don't we? We have feelings, don't we?"

She set Sophie down and began to scrub out the skillet. Immediately Sophie gave a loud, piercing wail. "Now, now, Sophie, no need to cry." Sarah Pearl picked her up and rocked her back and forth in her arms, trying to remember a little song about a treetop her mother had taught her. "Don't cry, don't cry, or I'm sure I'll cry too. Oh, I hurt so terribly. At least you've still got a mother and two brothers!"

"Want down. Want down!" Sophie struggled in her arms.

"All right—seems like nobody wants to be where they are. You're not the only one." Sophie immediately became occupied with crawling after a grasshopper.

"Now, don't wander off, Sophie, while I clear up here. Especially since I haven't done talking to you. You're the only person I can talk to. I don't care if your two-year-old brain can't understand what I'm saying." The toddler looked at her, puzzled. "And do you know what's worst of all? Well, your father just up and died, but he couldn't help that. My own father just up and left me, but maybe he couldn't have helped that. Isn't that something?"

But Sophie found the grasshopper more interesting and wandered off without even a sympathizing look in Sarah Pearl's direction.

At this moment Sarah Pearl's heart felt less like the leaden weight it had earlier and more like that burning fire under the grate. "There, take that! And that!" In anger and with determined emotion, she kicked dirt over the flames to quench them, wishing she could do the same to her emotions. She folded up the grate with a clang. In a vengeance she scoured out the skillet with sand, then almost threw it and the grate onto their hooks under the wagon axle.

"Go get the water bucket and don't forget the kettle either," she hissed to Tom, who'd just sauntered up. "Did that last time, remember!" He looked surprised, ducked his curly head, and ran off to find the water bucket.

Guilt immediately washed over her like a chilling rain. Oh, what had gotten into her? Taking out her anger out on that skillet, that grate. And now on Tom! Tom, who'd come all the way back on Boone to rescue her when she'd thrown herself out of the wagon, hoping to run back to Four Corners. After all, he'd saved her from bears and who knows what else. She had to admit that, if only to herself.

Mrs. Kerber suddenly stood before her. "We're ready to move out. You ss-sit up front on the wagon bench with Michael and Tom. And don't forget your ss-sunbonnet against the ss-sun. And take Sophie on your lap up there with you. It's going to another a hot day. I'm feeling tired this-ss-sss morning. I'm going to lie down and ride inside the wagon for a ss-spell. My old leg's troubling me."

No way was Sarah Pearl going to sit up there with Michael! Especially not after that johnnycake incident. "It's all right, ma'am," she said, trying to hide her anger. "I think I'll walk alongside. Those oxen go at such a slow pace—no trouble keeping up. I can carry Sophie on my back."

What a crazy decision. After about half an hour, she regretted it. By mid-morning the sun was hot and burning the dusty trail. She felt it penetrating the soles of her thin boots—already beginning to wear out. The vast, endless prairies seemed to dance up and down in waves of heat. And Sophie on her back grew heavier and heavier.

"Sophie want down," the toddler whined. "Wanna be wi' Mamie." She pointed to the wagon.

Around noon Michael drew up the wagon under one of the few stands of poplar trees they'd seen that morning. "Looks like a watering hole over there," he claimed. "Those oxen need watering, and a rest. Been pulling hard all day in this heat."

And Sarah Pearl, ashamed to admit it, was ready to give in. She was hot, tired, and horribly thirsty. The water felt cool and refreshing as she waded a little way into the pool, her blue and yellow calico skirt along with Mama's petticoat, tucked up around her waist. She didn't care if it was improper. Why did women have to wear long dresses, anyway?

Frogs leapt and splashed along the far edge of the pool, and dragon flies hovered with silver gauze wings over the tops of the reeds. The water smelled lucious, she'd almost forgotten the familiar smell of lakes and rivers. She pushed far back into a corner of her brain the painful association between rivers and Jason. At this very moment, the peace of this place and the refreshing spell of the water was soothing and exactly what she needed. She wanted to stand in this beautiful and soothing oasis forever. For a few precious moments, she had no thoughts of the Kerbers, not even of her father's disappearance.

With a jolt she realized Michael was leading the oxen back up from the watering hole. "Ready to move on," he called. "Got another ten miles or so to do today 'fore dark."

With a long, drawn-out sigh, Sarah Pearl waded out of the pool, climbed over the low bank and laced on her boots. Her stockings had already developed gaping holes, making the boots more uncomfortable than ever. Mrs. Kerber was about to climb back into the wagon to lie down.

"Oh, Mrs. Kerber," she called, "could I—would you mind—" and then broke off. About to ask whether she could ride with her inside, she realized it would be too cramped. Besides, the jolting was more uncomfortable there than on the spring-supported driving bench. Boone—couldn't she ride? And Tom could take Sophie with him and Michael on the driving bench.

"Tom," she started to ask, "how about—" But Tom had already unhitched the horse and was taking off ahead down the trail. But how about the oxen? She could ride astride Blue, the smaller one. She'd done it on Papa's ox, which he used for plowing, when she'd hike up her skirt and dig her legs into the animal's furry sides. No, she didn't dare try that with Blue. Michael would laugh at her for sure.

Now he was looking at her. "Miss, fill that last water cask," he demanded. "And then you can help me bolt this heavy yoke back onto the wagon tongue."

She felt a surge of anger. "I suppose you'll expect me to drive the wagon next?" She made no effort to disguise the acid in her voice.

"You must be joking," he sneered. "You couldn't manage these boys. Not in a million years. You'd let them take off. The wagon'd overturn, smash to smithereens—and then where'd we be, eh? Stranded out here in the middle of nowhere."

"Well, maybe that'd be better for me, wouldn't it? You'd like that, wouldn't you—you and your family?"

For a moment, Michael paused in what he was doing with the team harness. If she expected him to answer, she was disappointed. He said nothing, but finished—more slowly than necessary it seemed to her—threading the last line through the guide ring, then climbed up on the driving bench. Pulling his straw hat down over his forehead with a determined tug, he took up the reins in one decided gesture.

"Sarah Pearl," came Mrs. Kerber's hissing voice from inside the wagon, "I'd like you to take Sophie up there with Michael."

She had no choice. Angry and frustrated, Sarah Pearl climbed up on the bench, sat as far to the left from Michael as possible without falling off, and placed Sophie between them. Whatever she might say would bring some snide remark from him, so she said nothing for the next few miles. She concentrated instead on grabbing the side-arm of the bench whenever the wagon jolted over a hole in the trail, or making sure that Sophie didn't pitch forward and fall down under the wheels. Yet in one way, she would have liked to have talked to him. His father had died suddenly. Her father had disappeared suddenly. They had something in common. Surely that meant they had some feelings, some emotions in common. But how could she start? What could she say that he wouldn't dismiss with a snort or some implied ridicule?

What a relief, however, that Michael, for his part, focused on keeping the wagon on the trail, or chewing on the end of a wild wheat stalk. His only words "Gee" or "Haw," or "slow there," or just "Huh, huh," commands to the team. Sometimes it wasn't easy to recover the trail where the wind had covered it with debris, or the rain had washed out ruts from earlier wagons.

"Rolling hills," he said at last in his first comprehensible words. Pushing back his straw hat a little, he pointed ahead with the handle of his whip.

"What does that mean?" Sarah Pearl asked. "Let's hope it means the end of this terrible journey."

"Nope." Another long pause. "Done with this flat prairie for a spell, I reckon." He flicked his buggy whip.

"Well, what does that mean?"

Michael turned, fixed his cold gray eyes on her for a moment. He hesitated, as if considering whether or not it was worth explaining. Finally he turned away and flicked at the oxen again. "Means a river up ahead. Means a heap of trouble. May mean the end of our journey." He paused. "I hope you know more'n you seem to."

Chapter 3

THE CROSSING

A HEAP of trouble. "Why—" Sarah Pearl hesitated. She wanted to ask what kind of trouble. Why Michael was worried.

"You'll see—soon enough," setting his mouth in a hard line. He flicked the whip again over the oxen's rumps and looked straight ahead toward those low hills, rising up in the distance.

Something about Michael's tone—she didn't dare ask any more questions. Not that she didn't want to. There were a lot of things she wanted to talk about. Out of sheer loneliness, out of curiosity. Her own feelings. His feelings. Something told her he was hurting, as she was hurting. Taking a deep breath, however, she decided to try. "Say, how do you—I mean, what do you—no, I mean—"

"Watch out for Sophie, there," Michael interrupted rudely. "Can't you see she's falling asleep and about to slip off the bench?" He flicked the whip again.

No use, she thought. Any more talk was out of the question. She took Sophie in her arms, settled her on her lap, and tried to smooth down the toddler's dress and pinafore. Her pink sunbonnet strings had come untied again, and her precious small, rag doll, was about to fall out of the pinafore pocket.

Sophie began twining her little fingers in the end of Sarah Pearl's long braid.

"Sawah," she murmured, "Sawah hair—" Within a minute or two she wriggled closer against Sarah Pearl's shoulder, gave a deep sigh, and fell asleep.

There was a certain satisfaction in that closeness, in feeling the child's warm breath against her neck, her soft dark curls escaping from the sunbonnet and now brushing against Sarah Pearl's cheek. Sophie's small body snuggled against hers, as if needing comfort and protection.

At that moment, Sarah Pearl experienced something unexpected. Yes, she reflected, it was a strange feeling, mixed with what she could only describe as compassion for this child. She wasn't quite sure what that word, "compassion," meant, but she sensed it meant you pitied someone. Sophie's father was gone, in this case gone for good, and she would never see him again. Sophie was so young when he died, scarcely two. There was no way she'd remember him.

She glanced sideways at Michael, still staring straight ahead toward those hills, his mouth still held in that firm, straight line that seemed so unfriendly. The wagon seemed to be getting closer to those hills all the time. Its wheels turned around and around over the trail, just as Sarah Pearl's thoughts turned around and around in her head. Sophie had lost her father. Wasn't that true for Michael, too? She wondered how much he thought about his father. Was it more painful to have a lot of memories or none, like Sophie? Sarah Pearl had them.

And that strange voice she kept hearing—in the breeze, the creaking of the wagon boards, the rustling leaves—her father's voice—his Pearl—She suppressed a sob, an overwhelming urge to cry. What if—what if—what if she'd never see her father again? It was hard to believe that this Michael might feel any sympathy for her own situation. Oh, if only he'd say something. Something helpful. Anything.

Suddenly Michael turned and looked at her, a disturbed look on his face. Had he read her thoughts? She felt the heat rise to her cheeks and hoped her embarrassment wasn't obvious. Pulling her sunbonnet down more closely around her face, she leaned her head against Sophie's soft curls, where her sunbonnet had slipped away once again. Was Michael about to say something? Try as she might, she could find no words of her own to prompt him. They rode on another mile or two in silence, a disappointingly hollow and empty silence

During that long silence, Sarah Pearl wondered whether Michael was so locked up in his own feelings that he couldn't unlock them. Was he trying to unlock them during that puzzled look he'd sent her way?

Wasn't the difficulty of unlocking thoughts true for herself as well? Right now, with the heat, the jolting of the wagon, and the increasing heaviness of Sophie's body, it was too hard to work this out. Worse, still, her own thoughts were becoming more and more confused.

"Easy, boys. Easy now," Michael called to the team. The oxen had begun to snort and blow as they started up one of the larger hills. After a long, laborious climb, with a straining of every bit of tack and wheel and board on the wagon, they finally reached the top. Michael pulled back on the reins and set the brake. "Whoa! Ho, now. Whoo—aaah," he shouted, and pointed ahead with the whip handle. "There it lies! Down there—the James River!"

Sophie woke up with a startled cry and began to whimper. "There, there, Sophie," Sarah Pearl said, stroking the child's cheek. "It's all right. It's a big river ahead. Lots of water. Do you see it?" But Sophie buried her face against Sarah Pearl's shoulder and continued to whimper.

The trail fell away ahead of them, down a steep slope. And there, just beyond a band of willow trees, their gray-green spiky leaves quivering in the breeze, was a wide, fast moving river, sparkling between the trees. The smell of water touched her nostrils, disturbing yet welcome at the same time. At times she'd felt she was going to choke to death from the dust and the dryness of the prairie wind. Yet water for her inevitably held its own terror.

"Tom," Michael yelled, "get the wheel chocks out of the wagon and walk alongside! Not sure the brake'll hold us going down."

"What's happening?" Sarah Pearl was alarmed. "What do you mean, not hold us going down?" She shifted Sophie to the other shoulder and held onto her more tightly.

Disregarding her questions, Michael wrapped the reins around the bench arm and jumped down. "Maw," he shouted, "get out to help with the wagon. And you, Miss, just hold onto Sophie 'til I tell you otherwise!"

"But can't I get down? "

"Just do as I say," he ordered. "And keep Sophie out of the way!" He went around behind the wagon, but within a few moments came back with Mrs. Kerber. "Now, Miss, give Sophie to Maw—she'll lead her down to the river. Can't carry her because of her bum leg."

No time for questions. Sarah Pearl started to jump down off the bench.

Michael grabbed her arm. "No, no, you stay there. You're going to have to—" he broke off to say something to Tom.

"That's right, Tom, keep those ready." He turned back to Sarah Pearl. "You're going to have to work the wagon brake. Maw's not strong enough. And it'll take some doing."

"But I don't know how," she began, unsure of even her own strength or what he meant by some doing.

"Figured as much," he said, disgusted, "but no choice. Just grab this lever. Pull back to release, push forward to stop the wagon." He took her hand and placed it on the lever, closing her fingers firmly around it. "We got to ease the wagon down this slope. Tom'll keep the wheel chocks ready on the left side. I'll take the right. When I say, 'Brake off,' you push the lever back 'til we steady the wagon. Then we move a bit more 'til we're going too fast. When I say, 'Brake on,' you ease it forward. Got that?"

She didn't know whether she was more surprised to hear this many words from Michael—words which in fact suggested some show of confidence in her, or more nervous at what he was telling her to do. Both notions seemed related. No time to figure that one out, either.

"All right, brake off!" Michael yelled. The wagon didn't move. "Don't you realize, stupid girl, you've got to tell the team what to do? Got to say, 'Hupp—hoa—hupp!'" Then, grumbling to Tom, "Might've known. She's useless."

"Hupp! Hoa!!" she shouted, hesitantly at first, then a second and third time.

It worked. The wagon slowly inched forward until it began to roll down hill. Then a little faster. Michael began shouting, "Brake! Brake! But not too fast."

There wasn't much danger of that, though. It took all her strength to work the rough wooden handle, meant for a man's larger hand, and resisting any effort to move forward as if some live demon. With a scrapping sound, the brake lever bit into the wheel drums on the axles, and Sarah Pearl pitched forward, catching herself against the foot board just in time. At that moment, too, the wagon's wheels bit into the chocks pushed against them by Michael and Tom.

Again, "Brake off," from Michael.

This time the wagon gathered speed and pitched downward at an alarming rate. Now she knew to use both hands on the brake lever. She threw all her weight against it, and braced both feet against the front board. Again the brake lever bit into the wheel drums as she tried to steady her own forward motion.

"That's right—keep that up," Michael yelled.

After five or six combinations of brake, brake-off, Sarah Pearl felt the trail leveling out. It was no longer a question of going down, but whether to the left or right. There seemed to be deep ruts going off in both directions. She took the reins, which Michael had left wound around the seat rail, and tried to remember how it was behind Papa's plow.

"To the left!" Michael shouted.

"Haw! Haw!" To her amazement, the team actually did obey her command and veered left toward where the trail appeared to enter an opening in the trees along the bank. Just beyond that, she could hear the louder roar of rushing water.

Michael sprang up onto the bench beside her. "Give me those," he said, grabbing the reins out of her hands. "But you can brake when we get down to the bank." He said nothing the next few moments as the wagon rolled gently down the last bit. Once they drew up under the willow trees, he added, glancing furtively in her direction, "Couldn't have managed—" he stopped, undecided what else to say, even whether to offer a word of thanks. But then, "Brake here! Now I've got to figure out how we get across the James River."

"That water ss-ssure looks high, ss-ss-son," Mrs. Kerber remarked, shaking her head and pointing at the river with her awful cane. "Sophie, child, keep out of that water!"

Sophie started climbing among the willow roots. "No, no, Sophie," Mrs. Kerber cried. "Don't wander off, I ss-said!" Sophie was paying no attention.

"What do you think, Ma?" Michael asked. "Should we take the wheels off the wagon and float across?"

"Looks like we may have to. Done it before. They don't call thes-sse wagons prairie ss-schooners for nothing." She smiled faintly at her little joke. How weird, seeing that woman smile! Sarah found no humor whatsoever in those snake-like hissing sounds, no matter what humorous words they might have attached to them.

All the same, Mrs. Kerber looked worried, over and above her generally solemn expression. "It'll be a lot of work, though. Taking off all them wheels, putting them in the wagon. And can't always be ss-sure those oxen can ss-swim across." She shook her head again and looked off in Sophie's direction. "Sophie! That child! Won't ss-stay put for the life of her. Sophie! Come back here!"

Sophie had wandered closer to the bank, where there was a shallow sandbank. Clapping her hands, she exclaimed, "Cake," she said. "Make cake for Becky." She took out the doll from her pinafore pocket and propped it up against a willow root. Scooping sand into a pile with her hands, she started stirring it with a stick. "Dolly likes cake. Becky eat cake with Sophie."

"What were you thinking about the cross-ssing, then, Michael?" Mrs. Kerber continued.

He blew out a deep breath. "I recall all that work floating across, back there on the Ohio River. And we had Paw with us."

He looked thoughtful for a minute, as if remembering something he didn't want to think about. "But maybe we won't have to this time. Look out there—two channels. Seems like there's a sand bar in the middle. If we could just get across those two gaps. Don't know how deep—I'll wade out to get a better idea."

"Going with you," Tom insisted.

"No you won't. You stay here with Maw."

"But Michael—"

"No, I said." At this Tom looked disappointed and started kicking at a couple of rocks.

"That's-ss right, Tom," Mrs. Kerber said firmly. "Looks-ss too dangerous, even for Michael. Be careful, Michael—current looks-ss awful—"

Michael took off his boots, rolled up his overalls, and waded in a few feet. He steadied himself by hanging on to an overhead branch, but the branch only went out over the water so far. After that he had to struggle to stay on his feet.

"Only up to my waist here," he shouted about half way across. In an instant he stepped into a hole and went all the way under. When he surfaced a few seconds later, sputtering and pushing his hair out of his eyes, the current had swept him another yard or so down stream.

"If I can just make it to that first sand bar," he shouted. "Hard going, though." He slipped again, but managed to find his feet by thrashing his arms around.

Sarah Pearl held her breath. What if he went under and couldn't get back up? Could he swim? What if he drowned? If anything happened to Michael, she'd be stuck out here in the middle of nowhere with the rest of the Kerbers. What then?

"Oh, Mamie! Help! " Sophie's screams pierced the airs above the roar of the river.

The child had fallen into the river. "Sophie! Sophie—Mamie's coming!" Mrs. Kerber ran along the bank waving her hands in the air. "Sophie—Mamie's coming!" In the force of that emergency, there seemed to be less hissing in her voice. How strange that woman was! One minute like a witch, another like a . . . a . . . well, almost like a mother.

Despite Mrs. Kerber's warnings, Sophie had wandered upstream along the bank, away from her sand cake, away from the roots of the willow tree. She was now tangled up in some drifting tree branches caught in waterweeds at the edge of the bank. Desperately clutching dolly with one arm and hanging on to a thin branch with the other, she was screaming hysterically.

A loud crack. In horror, Sarah Pearl saw the branch break and plunge the water.

"Mamie! Mamie!" Sophie cried, as the current swept her slowly at first downstream along the bank, then more rapidly farther and farther out into the main channel. The broken branch she was hanging onto was hardly enough to keep her afloat. Only the air trapped under her dress and pinafore kept her from sinking, and that would soon be gone.

The scene brought Sarah Pearl a flash of images, a rush of horror. It was happening all over again. Her brother, Jason. His screams, her mother's helpless running along the bank. Sarah Pearl could not move. She was paralyzed with fright then and paralyzed now. She couldn't even shout a warning to Michael, who'd just reached the sandbar in the middle.

But Michael already saw what was happening. "Wait, wait," he cried. "I'll try to get to her. Stay right there—keep out of the water. Too dangerous."

"Let me try," shouted Tom. He started to wade out into the river.

"No, no, Tom! Stay there! Too deep for you!" Michael waved him back. "I'm closer."

By now Sophie was floating quickly toward Michael, her head just managing to stay above water. "Almost there, Sophie," Michael shouted as he pushed himself out into the current. Only an arm's length away, and she went under. Her little pink sunbonnet rose to the surface, swirling and bobbing along with the current.

"You, there!" Michael shouted in Sarah Pearl's direction. "Stop her! Do something!" What he said next was drowned out by Mrs. Kerber's incoherent yelling and Tom's panicked shouts as he ran along the bank, trying to keep up with Sophie's floating sunbonnet.

Suddenly Sarah Pearl saw a small hand rise above the water, then a pale, frightened face. Sophie was about three yards upstream and at least that far away from the bank. Sarah Pearl hardly knew what she was thinking, except she remembered how, that very morning, she'd experienced a sense of closeness to Sophie, a feeling of compassion. Almost as if she were her own little sister, the sister she'd never had.

In split-second flashes of memory, she recalled how she'd been able to turn her heart-sickness over her father's disappearance to into a kind of wondrous energy. And that energy had enabled her to maneuver the wagon down to the riverbank, something she never would have thought possible in a thousand years.

With the thought of that miracle, the miracle of wondrous energy, Sarah Pearl plunged into the current. In only seconds it came up to her waist. Her skirt felt heavy around her legs, dragging and sucking her down. If her boots hadn't been laced up over her ankles, they would have come off. But they were in the way and as if she had rocks instead of feet. With all her strength, with more strength than she would ever have imagined, she forced her body out toward Sophie against the rush of water.

"Sa-wah! Sa-wah!" Sophie screamed. Riding down on the current, she was almost within reach. Sarah Pearl lunged forward and held out her arms just as Sophie rushed past. She caught her—but only just barely—by the sleeve. There was a ripping sound, but it held.

The next instant Sarah Pearl slipped and lost her footing. Desperately she threw one arm around Sophie's body and tried to keep the child's face above water. With her other arm she thrashed water, kicked her feet, tried to find the river bottom again. All the while she was swallowing mouthfuls and feeling her lungs were about to burst.

There was a sudden jerk and a terrific pain at the back of her head. Someone had grabbed her long braid. She felt a strong arm come around from behind, around her neck, under her chin, raise her head far enough above the water so she could breathe. She gasped for air and spit out several mouthfuls of water.

"I've got you," said a voice. "Hold on to Sophie!" She was being slowly pulled backwards toward the bank as the water foamed and swirled around them.

Sophie was limp, her eyes tightly shut. Was she dead? Sarah Pearl hoped beyond hope it wasn't so. At the moment, though, her thoughts were more on finding the bottom with her feet and getting out of the river.

The strong arm holding her head above water suddenly slipped away. Once more she gasped and struggled to stay above the water.

"Oh no!" Michael shouted. "Lost—lost—my grip—wait—try—" He struck out after her, but the swift current had already pushed her too far ahead and farther out into the middle of the river.

Once more she was on her own. Her long skirt tugged at her body, threatening to suck her under, her boots weighed a ton. She couldn't let go of Sophie, which left only one arm free. Desperately she kicked and kicked in the direction of the riverbank and used her one arm as a kind of oar. She'd once seen somebody swimming in the lake near Papa's homestead cabin. It seemed to her that's what they did—using their arms like oars, like in a boat.

In the distance she heard shouts, her name, Sophie's name, Michael's name, her name again—Pearl—Puur-ull! She looked ahead to where she'd heard that voice. At a bend in the river, a dead tree had fallen across the bank and lay partly in the water. If she could only push her body closer to that curve, that tree, maybe she could hang on to one of the branches.

It seemed she was getting closer. Closer—just a few feet more. But then, in the next few seconds, her strength gave out. Her arms, her legs had no feeling in them. Her brain seemed to be going dead as well. Water came over her head and she couldn't breathe. Up again, she took a deep gulp of air, tried to keep Sophie's head above the water.

But next time she went under she knew she couldn't come up again. She felt Sophie slipping away and out of her grasp.

Then a feeling of something solid under her right foot. She struggled less against the current. Another strong force, a different kind of force. Strong arms pulling her up out of the water. It all seemed like in a dream. Nothing made sense except the feeling of being able to breathe again. And the heavy weight of her soaked dress clinging to her body. The weight of Sophie's small body which she still held tightly within one arm.

Someone dragging her up over a muddy bank and laid her on something. Soft, dry grass. Sophie was lifted off and laid down beside her. Still Sarah Pearl couldn't speak. It took every effort just to breathe, and when she did, there was a sharp pain in her chest. Someone raised her head up, and she began to cough up water. Someone rolled her onto her side. More water came up.

"Now for Sophie," said a voice.

After a moment, the little girl began to moan and sputter. Sarah Pearl turned her head to see Michael picking up his sister. She wasn't moving or even breathing.

Sarah Pearl knew she should try to say something. "Splut—splat—gasp—acchh" was all that came out.

"Here, I'll prop you up against this tree—you'll breathe better." Sarah Pearl felt Michael's strong arms under her shoulders, being dragged several feet along the grass, then her back pushed against the rough bark of a tree. Without saying anything, he picked up Sophie by the feet and shook her up-side-down.

After Sophie coughed, gasped several times, and began to cry for her mother, he said, "Now you hold her, try to keep her warm." He laid her down on Sarah Pearl's stomach, then stood up, rocked back on his heels, and looked down at them, sticking his thumbs into his belt. Water streamed from his hair, his clothes, splattering on her and Sophie. "Say, I'll swear, if you two don't look like a pair of drowned river rats!" He smiled, although to Sarah Pearl it looked more like a smirk.

Keep her warm, eh? thought Sarah Pearl. Well, that wasn't going to be easy. She couldn't help shivering continuously and intermittently coughing up greenish water.

Sophie moaned and began to cry. "Sophie cold," she said, "Sophie wet."

"Listen," said Michael, "I know that, but I can't do much 'til I can build a fire. And I can't do that 'til I figure out how to get the wagon across the river." He left them to walk along the bank a ways up stream, then climbed onto a large rock jutting out into the river. "Hey there—Tom!"

To Sarah Pearl's surprise, Tom, the wagon, and Mrs. Kerber were upstream on the other side, where she'd left them the moment she'd plunged into the water after Sophie. How did she come to be on this side? The only explanation was that Michael had somehow managed to swim after her and Sophie and catch up just before they came to that curve in the river where the dead tree had fallen, where she thought she'd heard her father's voice. Then Michael had pulled them through the current to the opposite bank and dragged them out of the water.

"I'm not about to risk swimming back across," Michael remarked after he'd returned to where Sarah Pearl and Sophie were lying on the grass. "Don't know where we'd be if—" he broke off.

If what? Sarah Pearl was thinking. Yet she knew what the *if* meant. It meant that, if anything happened to Michael, she'd be stranded here on this river bank with a young child. It meant that if Tom and his mother couldn't get the wagon across, or it got wrecked in the process, they'd all be stranded until help came along. And if no help came along soon, they'd all die.

To die out here alone—she couldn't hold back her tears and started to cry along with Sophie. "It's all right, Sophie, it's all right, darling," she kept repeating, pushing the hair out of the toddler's eyes, holding her more closely, trying to rub some warmth into her ice-cold hands and shivering body. Yet she was also vaguely aware that the comforting was directed toward her innermost self as well. She looked for Michael. She needed reassurance he was still there.

But Michael had other concerns at the moment. He'd returned to the big rock and was shouting directions across the river to Tom. "Now listen to me, Tom. I think the oxen can manage the two channels each side of the sandbar, if you keep them steady. You know you've been pestering me all along to let you drive. Well, here's your chance. You'd better make good."

"Leave the wheels on, you think?"

"Probably all right. Water's no more than neck high, both sides of the sandbar. You've got to watch out for any holes, though."

"Oh, Sophie, my poor little Sophie," repeated Mrs. Kerber, pacing up and down the opposite bank and wringing her hands. "Is ss-she . . . is ss-she—"

"She'll be all right, Maw," Michael answered. "Slightly the worse for wear—a bit water-logged. Lost her sunbonnet, her rag doll. That'll prob'ly be harder to take, I reckon."

What have I lost? Sarah Pearl asked herself. So much more than that. She hiccuped more greenish water and closed her eyes. If only her father had caught up with them back there on the trail. If only he were here. Oh, if only she knew where he was.

"You sure about the wheels?" Tom repeated.

"Should be fine. If you don't hit any big rocks, deep holes. And, Maw, you sit up there beside Tom, give him a hand if you can. Water may get into the wagon—can't help that. Make sure the bedding, flour kegs and all are put up high to stay dry. And don't forget to throw my boots in."

Sarah Pearl shivered with cold as she watched Tom and Mrs. Kerber get the wagon ready for crossing over. It seemed to take forever. Sophie snuggled against her, moaning, sniffing, crying about losing Becky, her rag doll. Maybe it was a little like herself, Sarah Pearl thought. All that self-pity. Couldn't she lose some of that? Michael's shouts snapped her back to reality.

"Little more to the right! Now the left! Watch out for that rock—that floating branch!"

"Hup—Haw, haw." Tom on the driving bench, his mother holding on desperately beside him, was already guiding the wagon into the water.

As she watched, it slowly moved through the first channel, then pulled up onto the sandbar in the middle of the river. After a pause allowing the team to rest, Tom headed the wagon down into the second channel.

"Now watch out," Michael called, "that gap's a bit deeper. Keep the team steady 'til you pull out onto the bank. And, Maw, be ready on the brake. Can't let the wagon roll back into the water. Tom, you'll have to help her. She hasn't much strength in her hands."

"Come on then, you beasts," said Tom to the team. The oxen were already puffing and blowing nervously and threatening to stop mid-stream. "Hup—Haw, haw," he kept repeating.

Finally Tom got the team to the bank, where Michael grabbed one end of the yoke and guided them up onto a level spot. "Brake now, Maw," Tom said. "Here, I'll help you. Made it," he shouted gleefully. "Of course, I knew all along I could!"

Some distance away against the tree trunk, wet, cold, and with Sophie lying against her, exhausted and still spitting up river water, Sarah Pearl watched the wagon's safe arrival. Hearing Tom's boast struck her with a moment of truth. It was so powerful that it drove away all feelings of the fear, pain and horror she'd just experienced.

Yes, she'd made it, too, and learned something about herself in the process—that was part of the pain. She'd managed to get the wagon down the other bank. She'd saved Sophie from drowning. That made two miracles . . . Well, three, actually, if you counted the fact that Michael Kerber had saved her from drowning!

Chapter 4

A Daring Plan

"WELL done, well done!" Michael slapped Big Horn on the rump and give Blue an affectionate rub on his broad muzzle. "Good boys, great beasts!"

The wagon, river water streaming off every surface, rolled to a halt in a small, level clearing along the bank. The oxen snorted and puffed, moving restlessly in their yoke as if considering they'd done enough and weren't ready yet to move on. And Sarah Pearl, sitting propped up against a tree where Michael had dragged her up over the bank, was of the same mind.

Still holding Sophie, who was whimpering, sniffling, and complaining about losing her doll, Sarah Pearl, shivered, miserably cold, wet, and exhausted. Although fragmented thoughts about the three miracles offered some consolation, she wondered whether she'd have the strength or the will to continue this endless journey. It was taking her nowhere. Nowhere was not where she should be if there was the chance her father had returned home. If that were the case, surely he'd be looking for her.

"Sawah—Sawah! Want go home!" Sophie, wriggling and squirming in Sarah Pearl's tight grasp, echoed her own feelings.

Michael seemed to be paying no attention to either of them as he unhitched the oxen and led them over to a patch of grass on the far side of the clearing. "Graze for a bit, boys," he said, with another slap on Big Horn's rump. "You made it. You did well today."

"They did, indeed," remarked Mrs. Kerber, as she shakily climbed down from the driving bench, placing her feet carefully in the wheel spokes. "And ss-so did Tom."

"Knew I could do it. Knew it all along. And I only got my feet wet—see?"

"Say, Maw," said Michael, suddenly kneeling on the ground, "More important than Tom's smelly feet, look down here!"

Supported by her cane, Mrs. Kerber took a few steps around the clearing. "Yes—wagon ruts-ss—remains-ss of a campfire. Recent, too. This must be where the main trail continuesss wes-ss-st."

"Seems likely," said Michael. "Suppose it could be the Johnson Train, just ahead of us? I seem to recall a river crossing just about here on Mr. Johnson's map."

"Let's-ss hope this-ss is-ss the one. But it'll be dark in another hour. We'll camp here for the night. Tomorrow, though, more ss-speed to catch up

"Won't argue with you there, Maw. Oxen aren't in any condition to move on just yet. Me neither." He glanced over at Sarah Pearl, still holding a wriggling Sophie. Gesturing with his thumb in their direction, he added, "Them neither."

"Build a fire then, quick as you can. You're all ss-soaked through and chilled to the bone." Coming across the clearing, she leaned over Sarah Pearl to raise up Sophie's head. "Oh, my poor little Sophie! We almost los-sst you!"

Sophie's answer was to cough and vomit a large quantity of water into Sarah Pearl's lap. The smell was nauseating.

"She's got to get out of those wet clothes-ss—and at once. Sarah Pearl, bring her over to the wagon."

By this time, Sarah Pearl was shivering so much that her teeth chattered. As she slowly got to her feet, her hands, feet, and brain were numb. Still, it was hard to disregard the feeling of resentment at Mrs. Kerber's apparent slight. Hadn't she just saved Sophie at the risk of her own life? Didn't the woman recognize that? Carrying Sophie as best she could, she numbly followed Mrs. Kerber across the clearing, where Michael was assembling firewood. He glanced at her as she passed. It seemed to her that he nodded slightly.

As they approached the wagon, Mrs. Kerber said, "Well yes-ss, you come into the wagon, too. Maybe I can find ss-something—" Turning toward Tom, she broke off to shout, "Tom! Don't forget to put the chocks under the wagon wheels."

Once inside the wagon, Mrs. Kerber unlocked the large trunk along one side and began taking out various items of clothing and bedding and shaking out their folds as she did so. "Sophie, here's your little green wool—the warmth should feel good. Sarah Pearl, take off her things-ss, wipe her down with this-ss towel, put this dress-ss and ss-stockings on her. This little ss-shawl for good measure, and tie it on tight around her waist. Then wrap her up in this-ss quilt."

Shivering the whole time, Sarah Pearl finally got Sophie dressed. All the while Mrs. Kerber was bent over the trunk, hunting deeper toward the bottom of the chest. At last the woman pulled out a dark wine-colored flannel skirt with a matching bodice, faced with shiny black material and a row of jet-black buttons. The pungent odor of camphor mothballs filled the air, adding to the smell of Sophie's vomit. A wave of nausea added to Sarah Pearl's discomfort.

"Here, this-ss may be too big, but it'll have to do. Be real careful when you walk, don't rip out the hem. You've got some ss-spare unmentionables-ss in that carpet bag of yours-ss? Good, I'll take it out of the trunk. Now, Sophie and me'll go back out to the fire so's-ss ss-she can warm hers-sself. You get dressed." She shut the trunk lid with a thud and locked it with a key attached to the belt around her waist. "And be ss-sure to wash out those things in the river and hang them on the bushes-ss. Michael's-ss, too," she added, as she took Sophie by the hand and proceeded to climb down from the wagon by way of the driving bench rather than the tailgate. Sarah Pearl had noticed quite early during the trek, that whatever infirmity Mrs. Kerber seemed to have, it made it difficult for her to enter or leave the wagon any other way.

The idea of now wearing something of Mrs. Kerber's was repugnant, even if the under garments—the unmentionables—were her own and between that dress and her body. She drew them out of the carpet bag, reminded for the hundreth time of her father, and how he'd carried that bag when he'd returned from the war. Her mother's silver locket slipped out from the camisole folds and dropped to the wagon floor. In a flood of emotion she picked it up and fastened it around her neck. At first she felt the shock of the cold chain, but warming it with her hands, it soon felt a part of her. She'd wear it now, always.

The fact that the silver locket and the white linen under things had been her mother's was strangely comforting. What a pity she'd had to leave her second-best, the yellow gingham, behind. Her pink silk best dress would be ruined for sure, out here in this wilderness. She didn't dare wear it, although she wasn't sure what she was saving it for. An inescapable thought—there might never, ever, be the need.

That evening Sarah Pearl was exhausted and feeling too nauseated to prepare any kind of a meal. After a rather sharp exchange of words, Mrs. Kerber, complaining all the while and accusing her of being lazy, reluctantly brought out some beef jerky and hardtack from the tin food canister. Sarah Pearl's stomach refused to consider it, although she accepted the mug of tea Michael handed her. He'd made it bitterly strong, and it set her teeth on edge. At least he'd offered to make it.

She now sat as close to the campfire as she dared, shivering, her stomach still producing little heaves from the tea. She'd wrapped herself in Mrs. Kerber's winter shawl, begrudgingly offered earlier it seemed, and wound it around Mrs. Kerber's ugly second-best dress. At least there was the secret comfort of her unmentionables underneath. She pulled a thick quilt over her knees, hunched over, and hugged them hard. The cold chill of the river, the frightening thought that she'd nearly drowned—along with Sophie—just like her brother Jason—refused to go away. More than ever it seemed they were coming from somewhere only to go nowhere.

"Best come ss-sleep inside the wagon again tonight with Sophie and me," said Mrs. Kerber, as she repacked what was left of the hardtack in the tin box and rose to leave. "We don't know quite what's-ss out there." Although this arrangement was nothing new—she'd usually slept inside the wagon with Mrs. Kerber and Sophie, while the boys slept outside by the campfire, on this night it was far from welcome.

"I'll come in soon," she said. She wasn't ready to lie down next to Mrs. Kerber on the wagon floor—not yet. She needed more space. She needed to think.

"Ahh—hmm," Tom yawned. "Think I'll just roll up in this here quilt under the wagon—'case it rains." He turned to follow his mother and Sophie. "Not that I'm scared of a little old rain, you understand. A man like me who can ford a big river with a wagon and team and all—"

Sarah Pearl remained alone near the fire, watching the sparks rise up as they danced along the smoke plumes and disappeared into the blackness above her. All around on bushes and lower branches wet clothes were hung to dry. She'd placed her button-up shoes as close to the fire as possible. There seemed little hope they'd dry out by morning. The leather had already begun to shrink and crack. Perhaps it was a kind of symbol of her unwillingness to come on this journey.

She pulled Mrs. Kerber's shawl more tightly around her, tucked the quilt firmly around her legs. It wasn't only a question of being chilled and exhausted. For some strange reason this night, her senses seemed acutely aware of everything. She could still feel the pressure of the cold river water on her body. Sophie's cries echoed throughout her brain. The flannel sleeve of Mrs. Kerber's dark dress brushed across her forearm. Her ears magnified the snapping and crackling of the campfire, just beyond her bare feet. Every spark, every night call of a bird, every whisper of the branches above her head, seemed vividly imprinted on her brain. Shutting her eyes, stopping her ears, had no effect. All were still there, whirling around in dizzy confusion.

A rustling behind her slammed into her thoughts, stopping them cold. A bear? That was the one animal she feared most.

"This'll build up the fire." Michael burst out from the edge of a stand of fir trees with an armload of wood. "Gathered up all I could find 'fore it was too dark to see. Hope this'll last the night." He threw down several thick branches, increasing that combination of sparks and hissing sounds. "You're not with Maw?"

"Later."

"Oh."

"I'm not ready for sleep yet."

"No?"

"My hair's still wet. I'm still cold." She'd undone her thick braids and spread her long hair out loosely around her shoulders. It gave her an unexpected, an unexplained sense of freedom. "How about you?"

"Oh, I'm all right."

They sat there together on the grass. Several minutes of silence ticked by, as if both of them were lost in personal thoughts, watching the sparks fly up, the embers turn red, then crumble into ashes. "I'm fine," he finally added.

"You were brave today." She couldn't believe what she'd just said. Complimented him.

"Wasn't much."

"You helped save Sophie's life."

"Pure luck."

"You saved my life, too."

He looked at her in the firelight, a strange kind of look. Still, though, he didn't respond.

"It's been a hard trek, so far." Perhaps if she changed the subject.

"Guess so," he shrugged.

"Long way still to go?"

"Maybe 'nother five hundred miles or so."

Her heart fell. So much farther to go. Every mile another mile away from Papa. "What's at the end?" She still wasn't convinced it could be somewhere.

"Homestead."

"What does that mean?"

"Means Paw was granted back there at the government office in Ohio about 160 acres. Some place in North Dakota Territory or Montana. Don't know exactly. Town called Discovery."

"What'll you do when you get there?"

"Discover something, I guess." He shrugged his shoulders, forced a wry smile at his attempted joke.

"Like what? Discover what?"

The smile fell. "Don't you ever stop asking questions?"

"Sorry."

After a long pause, "Take up farming, maybe." Another pause. "That is, if we ever get there."

Sarah Pearl fell silent. His last remark somehow voiced her own—if we ever get there. Yet she realized there was more to it than that. What was she going to do if she ever got there? Something urged her to ask him. "What about me?"

"Well, what about you?"

"I mean, I don't belong to your family. I've got to find my father."

He looked at her strangely again, as if he knew something she didn't, a secret he couldn't share. He poked at the fire with a stick, prodded the embers, threw on another log. At last, slowly and between his teeth, "That'll be your affair I reckon."

At that remark he stood up abruptly and pointed over to the wagon "You'd best turn in, Miss."

"My name's Sarah Pearl."

He ignored it. "Dark now, Miss. I'll fetch more wood to keep the fire going through the night. Might be wolves around, saw some bear tracks down by the river. Go on in with Maw and Sophie. But I'll take that quilt."

Reluctantly Sarah Pearl unwrapped herself and handed over the quilt. *No, please, no thank you*, she thought. As if she couldn't use another quilt during the night. It seemed to be turning colder with each passing day.

That night Sarah Pearl, tired and cold as she was, couldn't sleep. She lay next to Mrs. Kerber, with Sophie curled up between them, on the straw mattress unrolled for the night and spread over the wagon floor. It was crammed between the big chest on one side and clothes hanging on pegs across the wood framing posts of the wagon on the other. In the dim reflection of the campfire, they looked like people standing there, moving, as if they were alive.

Why was her body so tired, she thought, but not her mind—how could that be? It raced through question after question. Where was she going? What if her father was coming after her? How soon would he catch up? What if not until Discovery? That is, if they ever reached it. If only there was someway to get back to Four Corners. How far was it by now?

Let me see, she calculated, about ten days. Maybe they'd gone almost fifteen miles a day, sometimes a lot less. What would that be? Let's see—ten times fifteen is—? Never very good at math. Let's say they'd gone about a hundred miles. How long would it take her to walk that far? Could she remember the trail? But the first problem would be getting back across the river. Bears, wolves.

Beginning to feel tears forming at the impossibility of it all, she turned her face into the husk-filled pillow and choked back sobs so as not to wake up Mrs. Kerber. Impossible, yes, impossible—unless, unless—surely one could hope for a miracle. Another miracle. Like this morning.

Miracles—they did happen, didn't they? Then wouldn't Papa be pleased to see her? She'd turn in toward the cabin from the main road. He'd be out chopping wood. Then he see her, throw down the axe. He'd hold out his arms. "Why, my darling Pearl—where'd you come from? Welcome home ! Missed you!"

Right in the middle of this happily imagined scene, however, she couldn't put aside a dark feeling of doubt. It crept into her mind like the black snake she'd seen at one of the campsites—slithering under the wagon, flicking out it's long tongue as it twined through a wheel. Then striking out and catching a beautiful green grasshopper. It was such an ugly sight that she'd run behind the wagon and thrown up. What if Papa hadn't returned home? Wasn't coming for her?

The campfire outside reflected red flickers on the canvas covering across the top, and the reflections reminded her of Michael. What he'd said, how he'd said it—*that'll be your affair*. As if Papa was gone forever. Or, worse still, didn't want her to return. Did the Kerbers know something she didn't?

If only she weren't so tired. So tired that it was harder and harder to think. "Mrs. Kerber—" she began sleepily. But Mrs. Kerber let out a few hissing snores and turned over on her side. "Never mind, then," Sarah Pearl whispered. "Tomorrow. Tomorrow, Mrs. Kerber, I'll find out."

Next morning there wasn't much opportunity until the scant breakfast of bacon and johnnycake was over. "No, no," protested Mrs. Kerber in answer to Sarah Pearl's persistent questioning. "He was-ss—no, no, I can't tell you anything about your father. Don't pres-ss me." She set her mouth in a hard, straight line, and turned away.

"But you—and Michael—you must know something." She followed Mrs. Kerber persistently around the campsite as she picked up the last of the breakfast dishes and hung the kettle and iron grate on their hooks under the wagon. "No, I can't talk about it." Angrier now, Mrs. Kerber started kicking sand impatiently over the dying campfire embers. "Where's-ss Tom? He's ss-supposed to make sure the campfire's out."

"Please, ma'am—"

"No, I said. And ss-stop asking. It's in your own best interest. Now, girl, go find Tom." With that she abruptly picked up Sophie and set her on the driving bench. "All right, Michael. It's-ss already late morning. We're ready to leave. Just as ss-soon as you finish hitching Blue."

Well, that's that, thought Sarah Pearl sadly. *Won't get anything out of her, looks like, although it's clear she's hiding something.*

Thinking back to that day they'd left Four Corners, Sarah Pearl suddenly remembered something. Mrs. Kerber and Michael were over at the back of the store talking to Mr. Bergstrom. In kind of low voices, looking over at her now and then. She was sure she'd heard her father's name mentioned, William Lundgren. Yes, surely they knew something, something they were hiding from her. Mr. Bergstrom had told them something.

Maybe she could get something out of Michael. That'd be tough. She'd have to figure out the best way to get Mr. Silence to open up.

"Miss—riding in the wagon or walking this morning?" Tom asked. "I'm on Boone, so them's your choices."

"Walking, thank you." She needed to walk to think, to be alone for a while. Riding inside the wagon put her too close to those Kerbers—Michael, Mrs. Kerber, and Sophie, all on the front bench, talking about her no doubt. No, she'd follow along behind, even though her boots were still wet from the river yesterday and very uncomfortable, especially without stockings. She'd forgotten to pack an extra pair. The ones she'd started out in got so thin and full of holes that she'd burned them in the campfire three days ago. At least her blue-and-yellow calico dress and underclothes had dried after being spread out on the bushes overnight. What a relief to strip off Mrs. Kerber's old, much-too-big, musty-smelling things!

"Now, girl, make ss-sure nothing's-ss left behind," ordered Mrs. Kerber. "We need everything we got to make it through."

"Yes, ma'am," Sarah Pearl sighed. Didn't she always?

"Hup, hup! Big Horn! Blue! Move on!" Michael flicked his whip at the team, and the wagon shuddered into motion, slowly at first as it mounted the gentle slope up from the river. How different from that steep and dangerous descent yesterday! Once the wheels entered ruts cut deep into the trail, providing smoother surface, the wagon moved forward at a steady walking pace.

Before following the wagon up the slope, however, Sarah Pearl looked around on the grass, along the sandy riverbank, and where the campfire had burned out. Anything left behind? They'd already lost one of the cooking pots. Of course, she'd been blamed for it, even though it was Tom's fault.

Something caught her eye in a clump of bushes. Michael's gray flannel shirt, where she'd spread out the clothes to dry. It still felt damp. She'd throw it into the wagon once she caught up.

By now the wagon was quite a ways ahead. Sarah Pearl hurried as well as she could, her boots hurting terribly. Maybe not such a good idea, walking. She'd ask them to stop so she could climb in over the tailgate. How humiliating! Not much chance Tom'd let her ride Boone. Couldn't see him walking, no siree.

As she walked, holding Michael's shirt spread out a little to dry faster, an idea fell upon her like a ton of bricks. A plan. A bold and scary plan. Could she do it? A strange, tingling feeling at the base of her spine. Butterflies in her stomach. But would it work? And how to begin?

That night, lying in the wagon between snoring Mrs. Kerber and whimpering Sophie, Sarah Pearl lay wide-awake. It wasn't only because her blistered feet hurt terribly from the fact that the leather of her poor boots had shrunk and cracked in drying out. It wasn't only because she'd refused to shame herself by asking to ride in the wagon—certainly not on the bench beside Michael. And it wasn't only that it'd been a long walk along a hot, dusty trail. Over ten miles, she reckoned. Seemed more like a hundred.

No, there was another reason. Her plan. Mrs. Kerber earlier that evening, as they'd made camp, asked about Michael's gray flannel shirt. "Didn't you get it from the bush?" she said accusingly. "It was hung there to dry, along with his overalls-ss. As you can ss-see, he's-ss got those on now, but he decided he could wear one of his paw's ss-shirts, his boots-ss as well." She looked at him proudly. "Mr. Kerber's things nearly fit him now, you know."

Sarah Pearl hesitated. Should she confess picking it up and hiding it behind a chest in the wagon? "Thought you'd taken it, ma'am," she said lamely.

"Well, I never—" Mrs. Kerber sighed in annoyance. "Can't depend on you for anything, can I? Losing a perfectly good shirt like that . . ."

That was the last straw! After all the work she did, after getting the wagon down to the James River bank, looking after Sophie—saving Sophie! They never would have managed without her. Now she was sure she knew what she had to do. Impossible, maybe, but she had to do it.

That night faint light from the dying campfire, where Tom and Michael lay asleep wrapped up in quilts on the grass, flickered inside the wagon. Once again it made those bits and pieces of clothes hanging on pegs inside the wagon seem eerily alive. Mr. Kerber's old canvas jacket, his straw hat. Tom's spare overalls. Mrs. Kerber's winter shawl, her horrible black widow's bonnet.

Sarah Pearl thought of all the other things in the big chest. There was the carpetbag with her best dress. At the last minute she'd slipped in the heart-shaped locked her Mama had given her, just before she died. She was thankful she wore it now. Sarah Pearl also knew that in the chest was a leather pouch of money she'd seen in Mrs. Kerber's hand back at Bergstrom's store.

The problem was, however, that Mrs. Kerber kept that chest locked, the key always hanging on a loop from her belt. Now the belt along with her big apron hung on one of the pegs just above Sarah Pearl's head, moving slightly in the breeze as if Mrs. Kerber were standing there, arms on her hips, with her sour, disapproving look. Sarah Pearl shivered again. How to get that key? How to take out the money? Wasn't it rightfully hers for all her work as their servant?

Slowly, cautiously, she raised herself up on one elbow. Sophie stirred but didn't wake. Sarah Pearl sat up on the straw mattress, the straw rustling too loudly—it seemed —under her. If she could just get up on her knees, she could reach the key. A snort from Mrs. Kerber. Fortunately, after a suspenseful moment, she turned over on her back and continued snoring.

But then, a horrible realization! Even if Sarah Pearl managed to get that key, she couldn't open the chest. Its big brass lock was just above Mrs. Kerber's head. For sure she'd wake up and demand to know what Sarah Pearl was doing. Things were already bad enough with that woman. She couldn't risk it.

Crushed and disappointed, Sarah Pearl sighed and fell back on the straw mattress, clasping the silver locket around her neck, feeling its warmth in her hand. She'd have to wait 'til morning—or later. But the more she waited, the farther from Four Corners the wagon would be. Moving, moving, never stopping. Mile after mile. Her frustration kept her awake most of the night.

By the time morning dawned, Sarah Pearl felt exhausted, light-headed even. Once up, she went through her tasks in a kind of daze—cooking breakfast, getting ready to continue on the trail, keeping Sophie from wandering off, and making sure all was packed away.

"Ready to head out?" Michael asked, tightening the last team harness buckle. He seemed to be staring at her. "You all right, Miss?"

"I'm fine, thank you." No way would she even hint to him how she felt.

"Best ride in the wagon for a bit. We should be catching up with the Johnson Train fairly soon, I reckon. Means we need to make as much speed as possible. Since we're out of those river valley hills, prairie's stretching out, flat as a pancake, so the going might be easier."

"Tom's on Boone?"

"Tom'll scout on ahead." He smiled slightly. "Why he named that horse after old Dan'l Boone. Once he finds the wagon train, he'll tell them to wait for us to catch up. You riding in the wagon, then?"

"No, I'll—" She caught herself just in time. His remarks provided the very opportunity she wanted. "Well, maybe that'd be best. For a couple of miles, anyway."

She lay curled up on the folded quilts in a corner of the wagon as it rolled over the rutted trail. The sun beat down and the flat, endless prairies shimmered in the heat as far as the eye could see. Hardly a tree in sight, except for a clump of poplars or cedars here and there, popping up out of waist-high grass.

Slowly moving black specks way off in the distance. She knew they were buffalo. Tom said so. Michael had tried to shoot one for meat. Missed. So they stayed with tough, dry salt pork or bacon in the tin food canister, and even that was nearly gone.

Conversation between the Kerbers ahead on the driving bench droned on and on, but she only heard snatches of it—"See that . . . another hour . . . Indian Mound . . . Sarah Pearl . . . buffalo . . . don't know . . . watering hole ahead . . . Sophie don't . . . Tom on Boone . . . Johnson wagon soon . . ."

Sarah Pearl was thankful the pucker string was pulled tight through the canvas wagon cover between herself and the driving bench. Because she couldn't see them, they couldn't see her. She felt herself drifting off due to lack of sleep, the heat, the rhythmic motion of the wagon.

Sometime later, she suddenly jolted awake when a wheel hit a rock and shook the whole wagon frame. She must have dozed off for quite a while. The sky had clouding over and the air felt cooler. Her plan. She had to act fast, before they reached the watering hole they mentioned.

The lock on the chest caught her eye. No use, the key hung on Mrs. Kerber's belt during the day. The belt and Mrs. Kerber were on the other side of that canvas cover. All her well-earned money lay out of reach in that locked chest. How would she pay her way back to Four Corners?

She pulled out Michael's gray flannel shirt from behind the chest. Way too big, but it'd have to do. Tom's overalls hung on the peg—probably dirty and messy. He was a boy, after all. But they might be about the right size. Quickly she slipped off her dress and petticoat, then pulled on Tom's overalls. Yuck, dirtier than she thought. Michael's shirt had to be stuffed into them, making her look fat. Nevermind, it helped the disguise. She felt for the locket, making sure it was tucked well inside.

Boots? What for boots? Her own were hopeless. Michael's? They'd been thrown into the wagon just before the river crossing and still lay just inside the tailgate. Way too big—but what choice did she have? She stuffed them with a couple of rags. As an afterthought, she took down a canvas jacket from one of the pegs and slipped it on. Almost fit, must be Tom's.

Wouldn't this be considered stealing? Then she thought of the leather pouch of money lying deep down in the chest. She thought of her last ten or twelve days as a servant. No. She'd paid for everything. She'd almost sacrificed her life for Sophie's.

Her hair—couldn't much pass for a boy with two long, yellow braids down her back. Mr. Kerber's straw hat up there on the peg—she could tuck the braid up inside. But when the hat still came way down over her eyes, she realized she'd have to cut her hair. A box of cutlery beside the box of dishes—she knew it held a sharp knife.

Sarah Pearl sat down on the floor of the wagon, took the knife in one hand and her hair in the other. It wasn't easy to cut through the thick braid, but at last she managed to get through half of it, then the other half by switching hands with the knife.

Looking at those braids, she started to tear up. So many memories, Papa, Mama. Hair like Mama's. Her beautiful hair. But it had to go. She leaned out over the wagon's tail gate and threw it strand by strand into the tall grass beside the trail. In a sudden inspiration, she wadded up her yellow sunbonnet and stuffed it into Mr. Kerber's straw hat. It fit better, but wasn't very comfortable.

What else should she take? She grabbed a pillowcase off one of the pillows. Important to take her own clothes so as to leave no clear evidence of what she was wearing when she disappeared. Surely they'd try to trace her.

Food—she needed something. A chunk of salt pork remained in the tin food canister, along with some dried apples and a few left-over biscuits from breakfast. She stuffed everything into the pillowcase, including the knife. Water? Essential, but no way to carry whatever she could dip out of the water bucket wedged in beside the chest.

Now she was almost ready. But wait—Sophie. A sudden wave of emotion came over her, as unexpected as it was puzzling. She'd grown so fond of the girl, and Sophie of her. At night, lying on the floor of the wagon, Sophie often snuggled up to her, putting her little arms around Sarah Pearl's neck. "Sawah! Me want Sawah!" she'd insist, whenever Sarah Pearl rode on the driving bench with Michael, or was walking behind along the trail. She'd intended to make Sophie another rag doll, like the one her mother had once made for her. She could have torn off part of her shirt, used dried grass for the doll's hair, drawn on a face with a piece of charcoal. But there hadn't been time, and she'd been too preoccupied with her plan. Yet the thought of leaving Sophie wasn't a welcome one, and it was hard to explain why.

And there was another problem. How was she going to be able to get out of the wagon without anyone noticing? Untying one of the canvas flaps along the side of the wagon, she peered out the small opening. There wasn't much to see, just flat prairie everywhere. There was absolutely no place to hide. Unless—unless—

Shading her eyes and leaning out over the tailgate and looking ahead around the left side of the wagon, she saw, about a quarter-mile distant, a small stand of cedar trees. There were four or five in a clump, surrounded by some brush and tall grass. That was the answer. It was her only chance.

Just as they were about to pass that clump of cedar trees, Sarah Pearl took a deep breath and threw one leg over the tailgate. Hanging on with one hand, holding the loaded pillowcase with the other, she swung the second leg over and dropped down onto the trail. The impact knocked the wind out of her. Unable to move for several seconds, she wondered whether she'd broken something.

Fear of being discovered soon gave her the energy to roll quickly over and over into the tall prairie grass along the edge. Crawling on her hands and knees and dragging the loaded pillowcase from there into the bushes, she struggled to reach some low-hanging cedar branches. Once under cover, she cautiously raised her head just high enough to look down the trail.

The wagon was still moving. They hadn't noticed her jumping out. They weren't stopping. Not yet, anyway. As she watched, her heart in her mouth, the wagon disappeared around a bend in the trail.

What next? Should she try to make her way back east down the trail or wait? The problem was there hadn't been much cover for the past half-mile or so. She'd be exposed if the Kerbers came back to look for her. A few spatters of rain hit her face, the distant thunder rumbled. Not safe to be under a tree when there was lightning. Not safe to be out in the open, either. A real problem. With the storm coming on, it was already getting dark. Evening couldn't be far off, although she didn't have any way of telling the time.

Not that she expected escape to be easy. She just hadn't expected this kind of dilemma. It was her sore feet and Michael's badly fitting boots, however, which decided for her. For right now, at least, she'd curl up under this cedar tree, hoping the Kerbers wouldn't turn back to look for her. Good that Tom had ridden on ahead—he wasn't likely to come looking for her this soon on Boone, not like the last time. No, the Kerbers were fast going off toward their nowhere. It was a satisfying thought.

She bunched up loose cedar branches into a sort of bed under her and wove a few into the branches above her as a canopy. Suddenly hungry as well as tired, she took out the dried apples and a biscuit. Although a little dry with no water to wash them down, it gave her the illusion of satisfaction. Settling into the coziness of her cedar nest, she worked the pillowcase into a soft spot for her head, pulled Tom's canvas jacket more closely around her, and curled up into as tight a ball as possible. Within minutes she dropped off into an exhausted sleep, too tired even to think about what tomorrow might bring, only that it might bring her closer to Papa.

Chapter 5

AMONG THE BUFFALO

WHERE was she? What happened? Was she still in that nightmare? At least Sarah Pearl hoped it wasn't still the nightmare. It had been so full of terrifying things—monstrous buffaloes with black snakes' heads chasing her. Or floods rushing toward her through prairie grass, coming closer and closer—she was about to drown. So real it was—her face even felt wet.

Half-afraid to open her eyes, she sat up but hit her head hard against a tree branch. Now she remembered. After jumping out of the Kerbers' wagon, she'd found shelter under a bunch of cedar trees. The water on her face was rain from a storm during the night. Good thing her clothes stayed mostly dry, except for the bottom of Tom's overalls. Good thing, too, pulling some thick branches over her. Then she'd snuggled down under Tom's jacket, bringing the pillow case under it to keep dry. Too bad Mr. Kerber's old straw hat had gotten soaked and now looked so droopy. Her sunbonnet stuffed into it was also wet. Well, maybe the hat would shrink a little out in the sun and fit better.

Looking out through the branches, she was reassured to see it really was a bright, sunny day. The sky was cloudless and intensely blue. The buzz of grasshoppers, crickets, the whistling chuurrr of red-winged blackbirds attacking the grain heads on wild oats growing in clumps here and there seemed louder than normal. Green and golden prairie grass stretched endlessly in all directions, except for a packed-down pair of ruts made by wagons And the stalks between the ruts were broken off by oxen hooves.

Wagon ruts. The Kerbers' wagon! How far ahead was it? A more frightening thought—could they have come back to look for her? Suppose they'd already passed her, and now were returning eastward—the very direction she was heading?

Cautiously she crept out from under the cedars to examine the ruts. She sighed with relief to see only one pair. That meant they hadn't turned back. She was safe. For now, anyway.

The big question was, should she begin retracing the trail east? It didn't look like there was any place to hide, at least for the next mile or so. They'd sure spot her out in the open if they were anywhere close.

Well, she'd just have to risk it, and be quick about it. No time to lose in putting distance between herself and those Kerbers. Munching on the last biscuit from the pillow sack as she started walking, Sarah Pearl's only concern at the moment was keeping the trail empty—behind her as well as in front of her.

The sun got hotter by the minute. Michael's boots were much too big and rubbed painfully against her bare feet, despite the fact she'd stuffed in a couple of rags to make them fit better. Why hadn't she taken a pair of his socks as well? However, as uncomfortable as Mr. Kerber's straw hat was from being wet and a little sticky, she was glad she'd kept it. From the sun's height, she reckoned it must already be close to noon. Moisture from the recent rain on the grass sent up a steamy haze, reminding her she was thirsty.

"Oh—ha ha! That's so good!" She burst into laughter—not real laughter, fake impulses, covering up what she really felt. "Yes, that's good," she forced out a snicker. "After I nearly drowned in the James River from too much water, I'm about to die from not enough. Life is sure full of strange things."

Up ahead was a low outcropping of rocks with some bushes and a lone pine tree. She had to rest. Michael's boots were becoming too painful. The rags stuffed into them had packed down so much that now the boots were still too big. Better to go barefoot, as long as the trail didn't get too rough and she could walk on the trodden-down grass part of it.

The first thing she did when reaching the rocks up ahead was to sit down and take off Michael's boots. She threw them, one by one, into the long grass well off the trail. The cool stone felt so good against her bare, blistered feet. Next to her left hand she noticed a slight depression in a large, reddish stone, still filled with rainwater. Lying on her stomach she plunged in her face and drank, came up for air, drank again and again. It tasted a little bit like sulphur, but it was nevertheless still water. Extracting the last piece of salt pork from the pillowcase, she washed it down with more sulphur-flavored water.

"What am I thinking of?" she asked out loud of no one in particular. "Sitting when I should be moving. And fast. First, though, let's see where I'm going."

Climbing up to the top of the rocks, she shaded her eyes against the sun with one hand and looked as far as she could in all directions. A distant rumble of thunder. Strange, couldn't be a storm coming. Not a cloud in the sky. Then, there, far off in the distance, a bunch of black specks—a huge herd of buffalo. They seemed to be moving southward. Hundreds of them, seemed like, their hooves booming against the ground and making it shake like an earthquake.

She didn't see anything else moving, except a faint breeze stirring the pine needles. A good thing. She sighed with relief to see and hear only the natural life which belonged on the prairies. And, for the moment, at least, it belonged to her.

By late afternoon, Sarah Pearl had walked as far back east along the trail as the Kerber's last campsite. At this rate, she realized, she might actually make better time than the Kerbers' wagon with its slow-moving ox team. Yes, that was where they'd camped night before last, in a shallow gully just off the trail. Looking around the campsite reminded her of events this morning and events last night. Mrs. Kerber's words came back to her, or rather her refusal to provide words. That refusal had been Sarah Pearl's breaking point. If she'd had any doubts, any hesitation at all, about leaving the Kerbers and making her way back to Four Corners and her father, that incident clinched it. If her father was still missing, she'd go in search of him. If by some wonderful chance he was now on this trail, coming towards her and closer every minute, well then, she'd meet him that much sooner.

A blackened spot in the gully marked the place of their campfire. She poked at it with a stick, hoping some live embers still remained. Nothing but cold, gray ashes. No way to start a new fire. It'd be a cold night, for sure, and she wasn't looking forward to it—in her bare feet and with only Tom's jacket for protection—and Mr. Kerber's soggy, straw hat.

She made the decision then to keep on going as far as she could before dark and risk finding a safe place to sleep farther down the trail, hopefully a nice old tree. Tom claimed bears didn't climb trees. Couldn't be sure of anything Tom said, though. Besides, there weren't all that many trees around until the hills around the James River and that was another whole day's walk. Then the James River. She shivered, just remembering that incident. How to get across this time? Must be another way. Or another miracle.

"Got to keep going," she said to herself, over and over again in a kind of chant. "Keep going—going—going." And so reluctantly and with a great deal of apprehension about what was yet to come, she left the cold ashes of the campfire and headed on down the trail.

What's that?" she cried. Just at the moment when it was almost too dark to see the trail any longer, just when she'd almost given up finding a safe place to sleep, she saw a faint glow ahead. Was it a campfire? The Kerbers? Retracing the trail? Maybe it was another family, a wagon train. She'd make for it. Food, a warm bed. Safety. She began to run.

The next minute, however, she stopped dead in her tracks. Who were those people? Friendly? Or not? She wondered if she should risk it. Something deep inside her whispered that she had no choice, as cold and hungry as she was. Then, there was also the matter of bears prowling around, coming after her. She had no protection.

By this time her pillow sack was empty of food and held only her dress, the soggy sunbonnet, and the knife. Should she keep them? Not knowing quite why, she decided against it. With the knife she dug a hole in the soft earth just off the trail. Then she pushed in the sack and scratched earth and pebbles back over it. But the knife she slid into an overalls' pocket—no telling when she might need it.

In spite of the growing dusk, she found she could follow the trail by feeling for the ruts with her bare feet. And the trail was heading right for that glow in the sky ahead and the smell of bacon.

Quickly it got pitch dark, as dark as a black velvet curtain stifling her. She couldn't always be sure she was on the trail. Several times she stumbled over rocks, loose roots, or found herself wandering among waist-high grass. Once she walked through what she knew was a skeleton—she couldn't tell whether the bones were human or not.

Didn't matter—it was a horrible feeling. Once she was sure she came across a broken wagon wheel, left by passing earlier settlers. At least that was a sign she was on the right track. The orange glow got brighter. The smell of bacon stronger.

She could hardly wait to get there—she hadn't had anything to eat since early afternoon—the last of the salt pork washed down with rain water. She stumbled on a rock. Her right foot came out from under her.

Suddenly she had the sensation of being swallowed up in that black velvet curtain, of not being able to breathe. She tried to scream but no sounds came. A flash of light exploded inside her head. Then blackness that went beyond the darkness of the velvet curtain and the night. Strange dreams took over, many of them, dreams turning into fragmented images, disconnected, terrifying. Would they never end?

"Well, bless my soul! Lookee here!"

"Find somethin', Jake?"

"Down there, bottom of that there ditch—"

Sarah Pearl opened her eyes. It wasn't dark anymore. So it must be morning. She became aware of two heads looking down at her, but with the sun behind them, they were just black blobs. And the sun hurt her eyes so much that she closed them and turned her head. It hurt so much she moaned in pain.

"Alive, you think? Saw it move, thought I heard somethin'."

"Can't be too sure. May have to bury him. Good thing he's already in a ditch. All's we have to do is shovel more dirt down on top of him and that'd be it."

"Well, don't just stand there. Better find out first. Besides, he might have something valuable on him."

"I say, there, boy. You dead or alive?"

"Umm—mmm—ahhmm—" Sarah Pearl couldn't seem to talk. Her tongue stuck to the roof of her mouth. She opened her eyes again, little by little, and moaned. A man with a bright red beard and wild-looking hair was leaning over her.

"This un's alive, Sam. What'll we do with him? Can't leave him here. Ain't decent, like."

"Well, bring 'im up outta that ditch. Then we'll decide."

Pain shot through her body as the man lifted her up. For sure this time she'd broken something. She felt herself being carried up the ditch, then handed to someone else who lifted her up and carried her a ways before laying her down on some grass. The grass felt cool and soft and smelled good as it tickled her nose. She just wanted to fall asleep again. Sleep—rest—

"Well, now what, Jake?"

"Dunno, Sam. I'll go ask Randy. He's back there at the watering hole with the horses."

Sarah Pearl heard voices, men's voices, as her mind drifted in and out. One of them sounded like Papa. Of course, he'd come to look for her, to take her home. "Papa? Oh Papa," she said faintly.

"Ain't yer paw, boy. Say, Jake, he's comin' to."

"Give him a swallow of water outta your flask, then."

She felt an arm under her head, raising her up. Something soft and leathery against her mouth, water being poured down her throat. She gasped and choked.

"Hey there, boy. Not so fast. Take it slow and easy That's right, right. One sip at a time. Feelin' better then?" He slowly eased her head back down on the grass.

Now that her head had cleared a little—although it still ached, Sarah Pearl began to realize her situation. She must have fallen into some ditch last night in the dark. These men, whoever they were, had found her. And they thought she was a boy. Of course. What else? She'd cut her hair, was wearing Michael's big, loose shirt stuffed into Tom's overalls. She'd buried her girl clothes. She wasn't sure about Mr. Kerber's hat. It might have been lost last night as she stumbled along the trail. Now she was sorry she'd thrown away Michael's boots, although her feet were probably so dirty by now these men might not notice they were a bit small for a boy.

"Randy says he'll be up directly, Jake. Says he'll have a look at the boy."

"Here he comes. So, Randy, what d'ya think? Leave him here?"

"Wouldn't be right, I'm thinkin'," said the man called Randy. He had a loud, rough voice, but what frightened Sarah Pearl more was the big, black hat he wore hiding most of his face. "Can't rightly leave him here to die slowly from thirst and starvation. Unless we shoot him first to put him out of his misery."

Surely they weren't serious? Now Sarah Pearl was really frightened. How could she have gotten into such a situation? Far, far worse than the Kerbers. In fact, by comparison the Kerber family was beginning to look kind and caring. "Oh, sir," she stammered. "Sir, I want—"

"Makes no difference, boy, what you want," said Randy. "It's what we want, eh, boys?" They muttered agreement. "Now then, how'd you come to be in that there ditch?"

Should she explain the whole story? She realized that wouldn't do. They might offer to go back down the trail to return her to the Kerbers. That'd be bad enough. Worse, however, were other possibilities. She shuddered, thinking of what it might it be like if they thought she was a girl, not a boy.

"Well, sir," she began hesitantly, "I fell out of—" No that'd give it all away. Back to the Kerbers for sure. So instead, she added, "You see, I fell into the ditch in the dark."

"How'd you come to be wanderin' alone in the dark in the first place?" The one named Jake. He seemed kinder than the other two, although his flaming red hair and beard were rather frightening.

"Well, you see, folks all lost. Left on my own."

"On your own? How'd that happen?"

"They were all—" This was getting more difficult. She paused for a moment, thought hard. "Well, they were all lost in the river." That was partly true, wasn't it? Lost for a short time in the river, at least.

"And you got this far on your own?" Jake sounded incredulous.

"Yes, sir. I'm all on my own now." She tried to look heartbroken. That wasn't difficult, under the circumstances.

"Well, I never," commented Sam. "Boy shows a lotta courage, don't cha think? Might be useful."

"I dunno," Randy said doubtfully. "Can you shoot, boy?"

"No, sir."

"Ride?"

"Oh, yes, sir, I can ride. Brake a wagon."

The men laughed. "We got us only three horses. Aint got no wagon."

"Useless, like I said," Randy put in. "Plum useless."

"But—" She thought fast. "But I can cook, sir." They looked surprised.

"Cook?"

"Yes, sir. Johnnycake, biscuits—a whole lot of things. Didn't have a maw, you see." And that much was true.

"Well, if that don't beat all," said Randy. "A boy who cooks? If'n that don't beat all."

"See," said Jake, "he might be useful. Gettin' awful sick of your grub, Sam. Makes me puke, just thinkin' of it. Shouldn't we take him along?"

"Dunno," Randy answered. "With only three horses, not much in the way of vittals to cook with in the first place."

"He can ride up behind me," said Jake. "Blaize can take the extra weight. And this kid looks kinda puny, like."

Randy hesitated, paced up and down a little. After a few minutes he said, "All right, then. But remember, you're responsible for him, Jake. Least sign of trouble, you know what to do. And that goes especially for the next buffalo drive. A herd spotted goin' south, five miles this side of Fort Rice. Can't lose any time goin' after 'em." Now let's saddle up and get movin'!"

So these men are buffalo hunters, thought Sarah Pearl. That was bad enough. What was worse was the fact that they seemed to be heading west, the opposite direction she wanted. If she stayed with them, she'd actually be retracing her steps— back in the same direction as those Kerbers! What if they met up? That'd just be the end . . .

And as if all that wasn't bad enough, she now needed to pass herself off as a boy. What if they discovered the truth? Out of the frying pan into the fire, as Papa used to say. And, speaking of frying pans, she wasn't that good a cook yet, either. At least according to Michael and Mrs. Kerber.

No, this wasn't good at all, but she had no choice. She was helpless in the hands of these rough-looking buffalo hunters who seemed ready to do away with her for no reason at all.

"Say, boy," Jake asked as he reached down and with the strength of one arm pulled her up behind him on the saddle. "What's your name? Can't go on callin' you 'boy.'"

What she really wanted to say raced through her head. No, sir, do please keep calling me boy. Instead she said, after a second or two of hesitation, "William, sir." That was her father's name. If her father was gone, she could at least carry his name along with her. "Folks call me Will."

"All right, then, Will. Hang on for all you're worth. Old Blaize here has got to make fast tracks to keep up with them buffalo."

For some distance they galloped along the main wagon trek west. Oh, thought Sarah Pearl, if only this bouncing around didn't hurt her head so much. If only Jake's jacket, which she had to hang on to for dear life, didn't stink like sweat and tobacco and whisky and she didn't know what else. If only they didn't run into the Kerber wagon up ahead. If only—if only—

Yet she wasn't sure what else the "if only" might be. Things weren't turning out at all like she wanted. Yes, into the fire, all right. After about a half-hour the buffalo hunters turned off the main trail and headed directly into the sun, due south across the prairies.

"Waterin' hole 'bout a mile up ahead," shouted Randy. "Stop there for a spell, but no longer'n necessary. Take some vittals." Sarah Pearl panicked. Her first test as their cook.

She needn't have worried, however. No sooner had they dismounted, loosened the saddles, and led the horses into the shallow pool of water, than Randy said, "All right, then, boy. You see that saddlebag on Sam's horse? Just pull out a bit of hardtack, some of that smoked eel. No time for cookin'—not 'til tonight. Then maybe you can cook us some big, juicy buffalo steaks, eh, boys?" The three men laughed, Randy slapped his thigh.

Pearl took out a bandanna wrapped around the hardtack and smoked eel, and spread it out on the grass beside the watering hole. The men snatched up most of it while taking care of the horses, adjusting the saddles, and reloading their rifles and pistols. That was all right, though. Her head still hurt too much for her to feel hungry. Besides, the sight and smell of the smoked eel made her feel a little sick, and the smell of Sophie's vomit came back to her.

After she tucked the now empty cloth back in the saddlebag, she went over to where a trickle of spring water fed into a creek running down into the watering hole. Lying flat on the bank, she drank as much as she could before Randy came over. His huge shadow fell menacingly across the creek.

"All right, then, boy," he said roughly as he shoved her shoulder with the toe of his boot, "on your feet. No more. Git movin'."

"Up here, Will," called Jake. "Git yourself up here behind me—pronto!"

Now they were on their way again, riding hard over rough prairie, which sometimes caused the horses to stumble dangerously. It was all Sarah Pearl could do to hang on to Jake. Occasionally they crossed the faint marks of tracks and each time Randy slowed the horses as if taking his bearings.

Once he stopped, got off his horse, and knelt down to examine the ground. "Ah hum," he said. "Lookee here. Thought so. Pony tracks."

"Shakota?" asked Sam, looking alarmed.

"Yup. Them Indians from the village just north of here passed this way for sure—and not too long ago. They may be after that big herd of buffalo, too. Come on then, boys. No time to loose. We got to beat them to it." He quickly remounted. "And now you listen here, Jake. That boy gets too heavy, slows down that horse of yours, off he comes. He'll just have to wander around the prairies on his own, like he been doin' afore we found him."

"But Randy—" Jake started to protest.

"You heard me. Then if'n them Shakota find him, let them take care of him—their own way!" He laughed a snarling kind of laugh. "Maybe he could talk his way out of it by offerin' to cook them johnnycake, eh boys?" Another laugh, echoed by Sam.

Sarah Pearl hung on desperately to Jake's jacket. She had to put both arms around his waist whenever they reached an open, level space and Blaize broke into a frantic gallop to keep up with Sam and Randy. She had to jam Mr. Kerber's straw hat tightly down on her head, just to keep it from flying off. Fortunately Jake had found it in the ditch with her. The rain had caused it to shrink a bit more. Now it almost fit.

"You wouldn't just leave me out here, would you, sir?" she felt compelled to ask Jake once she had enough breath to talk.

But the next instant they broke into another wild gallop, preventing Jake from answering. A wide ravine suddenly opened up in front of them, and Randy pulled his horse up short. "Horses'll have to pick their way down," he said. "Careful on the way up. Can't can't risk lettin' 'em break a leg, either."

Sarah Pearl seized this opportunity to repeat her question. Jake seemed to concentrate for a few minutes on getting through the ravine. Finally, in a low voice so that Sam, riding just behind him couldn't hear, he replied, "Might have to, Will. Wouldn't want to, but—but you know, Randy's the boss. Tell you the truth, though, I'd rather shoot you than let you fall into the hands of them Shakota. It'd be an act of mercy, I reckon."

Sarah Pearl shivered. She'd heard things. Murder. Torture. Hardly realizing what she was saying, she answered slowly, "Maybe so, Jake. Yes, maybe I'd want you to do that."

By late afternoon they still hadn't caught up with the buffalo herd. Sometimes they'd spot a cloud of dust way off in the distance, hear the faint thundering of thousands of hooves. But by the time they'd galloped hard toward the spot, the herd would be behind the next hill, or hidden in a deep ravine, or stampeding across a wide open stretch of prairie miles and miles away.

"Dang it all," Sam snarled as they paused to rest the horses. "Jest look at them beasts go. Never will catch up, seems like."

"Horses pretty darn winded as it is, all lathered up." Randy spat out a mouth full of chewing tobacco in the direction of a clump of sage bushes. It spattered the delicate gray-green leaves with ugly brown clumps. He narrowly eyed Jake's horse. "That horse of yours lookin' all done in. All that extra weight."

"Blaize's doin' all right. Just needs to catch his wind," said Jake defensively.

"Told you that kid means trouble," Sam remarked. "Best get rid of him now."

"Be fine, I tell you."

"You'd better be right," Randy cautioned. "We got to move on—and I mean now. Gettin' dark in an hour or so. Those buffalo, you know—they slow down and graze just before sundown. Don't move during the night. If'n we can get 'em in our sight by then, camp the night, then—"

"Start shooting first thing come dawn, eh?" Jake asked.

"Yup, piece of cake," Sam put in with a smirk. "Can take hundreds—if our ammo holds out."

This disturbed Sarah Pearl. She could visualize the terrible slaughter of these creatures—hundreds of them. Wonderful beasts—huge, noble, their great heads surrounded by massive amounts of dark brown fur, their large, sad eyes. Some of them with great golden horns. And what would these hunters do with all those buffalo? They couldn't eat more than one at a time. She'd heard the pelts brought good prices back east. But how to get hundred of pelts back there? These were only three men, on three horses. And she sensed that Blaize was already tiring, stumbling more often, snorting. Jake would have to drop her off and leave her there in the middle of nowhere any minute. In the midst of the Buffalo. In the path of the Shakota..

To her great relief and after only about a half-hour's ride, Randy pulled up short. "Make camp here for the night," he said, "I can see them buffalo down there in that valley grazin' away. Jake, scout around, shoot us a rabbit. Juicy buffalo steaks'll have to wait." He laughed. "Now we'll see if that boy can prove worth his keep. Boy—" he pointed in Sarah Pearl's direction, "we'll be expectin' some tasty rabbit stew afore long."

Sarah Pearl's heart sank, and she broke into a cold sweat. She wasn't sure she knew how to make rabbit stew. She'd watched Mrs. Kerber do it once, but—

Shortly afterwards there were a few gun shots and Jake returned, holding up a large gray rabbit by it's hind legs. "Got one for ya, Will."

"But I'll need—I can't—"

"Look, I'll make the fire, skin the rabbit. Then you can just roast it on some spits. I'll find some green branches for that. Salt's in Sam's saddle bag. Needin' anything else?"

"Nooo—guess not," she answered hesitantly, grateful for Jake's help. In fact, if it hadn't been for Jake all along— Now she'd just have to wing it. Her mind considered what came first. How did one get the rabbit onto the spit? Then what—

Suddenly a blood-curdling yell from over behind a group of fir trees, a rush of horses and men. Something came riding right through the fire Jake was making within a small ring of stones, scattering stones and burning wood fragments.

"Shakota!" screamed Jake, falling on his back onto the grass. "Randy—the guns—Will—watch out—"

Sam shouted something as he ran over to where the horses were tied to a tree branch. He snatched a rifle from its saddle holster and threw it to Randy as he drew a pistol from his belt. An arrow hit his hand, knocking away the pistol. "Take cover! Take cover!" he shouted, ducking behind the horses.

Now Jake was shouting at Sarah Pearl as he grabbed her by the legs, pulled her to the ground, and tried to shield her body from a flurry of arrows, which stopped after a few seconds. "They're more interested now in our rifles, the horses," he whispered in her ear. "Now's your chance, boy! Run! Will, run for your life! Get off into those bushes, hunker down, and hide!"

"But Jake—" she hissed. "They'll get you next."

"Maybe, maybe not. Only two or three of 'em, braves on ponies, see."

"Can't leave you—Blaize—"

"Don't be stupid, boy. Now's your chance. Randy—he's willing to—don't you see—"

In a flash of truth, Sarah Pearl understood what Jake was trying to tell her. It was most likely as dangerous to remain with the buffalo hunters under Randy's control as it was to be captured by the Shakota. And now Jake was offering her the chance to escape both.

Over by the horses Sam and Randy were fighting with the Shakota braves who were trying to untie the horses. One Shakota fell to the ground. She couldn't tell whether he was dead or alive.

Sam was bleeding from a gash in his forehead and a shattered hand. She couldn't be sure about Randy. He seemed to be trying to aim his rifle, but the brave kept wrestling it away. Jake lay moaning beside her. He'd been shot in the arm by an arrow, with blood now soaking through his canvas jacket. There were beads of sweat on his forehead, streaming down into his red beard.

"Jake—oh Jake—"

"It's all right, Will," he answered weakly. "I'll survive. Been through worse. You, now—you must do as I say."

"No, I—"

"Will! You heard me! Git—git away, before it's too late." He moaned and rolled over onto his wounded arm. "Pressure'll stop the bleedin', I hope. But here—take this—" he reached into his shirt pocket and handed her a small leather pouch. "Take—take it—might be useful—now git—git out—of here—"

Holding the pouch tightly in her right fist, she wriggled her way through the long grass to a clump of bushes about twenty feet from where Jake had started the campfire. Behind her the noise of the fight—shouts from Sam and Randy, the strange cries and whoops of the Shakota, screams and whinnies from the horses—rose and fell. Once under cover of the thick bushes she gasped for breath, not daring even to look back as she pushed Jake's leather pouch down deep into her overalls pocket.

A few moments later there was silence. What had happened? Were the hunters still alive? Should she go back? Run away? Before she could decide, however, she saw the hooves of horses coming through the grass toward her, the sound of words she couldn't understand. Both stopped. Silence again. She pressed her eyes shut.

Then she felt the sharp tug of someone pulling her up by the straps of Tom's overalls. Her own weight caused painful pressure across her bottom, between her legs. There were more unrecognizable words, laughter.

One of the Shakota was lifting her up, actually dangling her off the ground by her overall straps. Facing her was another Shakota on a pony, a cascade of black and white feathers falling down across his shoulder, bare arms sticking out of a vest which seemed to be made of feather quills and colored beads. He was laughing and saying something as he pointed to her straw hat. At that, the brave who was holding her suspended by her overall straps let go and she dropped to the ground. The fall knocked off her hat, and the Shakota laughed again as he pointed to her yellow hair. Both men exchanged some agitated words, gesturing first toward her, then back in the direction from which they'd come.

Then Sarah Pearl realized the man with the black and white feathers was leading not only Jake's horse, Blaize, but the other two horses as well. There was no sign of the buffalo hunters, no sounds from the campsite.

"Go," he said gruffly, pointing first to her, then to Blaize.

Sarah Pearl found herself swept up and swung over by her overalls straps onto Blaize's saddle. The weight of her body against the crotch and her bum was painful. Her hands were quickly tied to the saddle horn by rough leather thongs. More pain.

"Go," the man repeated, leaning close to the ground to pick up Mr. Kerber's straw hat with the point of an arrow, then waving it in the air like some sort of trophy.

With a kind of cry, the Shakota urged their ponies forward. With them came the three buffalo hunters' horses. And on Blaize came Sarah Pearl with no choice but to follow. To where? Her mind went numb, like her tightly-bound hands. All she could think of was, *to where*? To another nowhere?

Chapter 6

Dangerous Ways

SARAH Pearl had no idea how long or how far they'd ridden. Her numbed brain wasn't functioning. The sudden shock of the attack, Jake lying bleeding, Sam and Randy fighting to save themselves and the horses. She didn't know what had happened to them. Only one thing was certain. After the Shakota caught her trying to escape, they put her on Jake's horse and tied her hands so tight to the saddle horn that they were numb, too.

The two Shakota were riding their ponies and leading the other two horses through most of the night, and the night was lasting forever. She was aware only of an occasional bright, silvery light when the moon came out from behind some clouds, or when low-hanging branches brushed against her face.

At last they came to a place were bright moon light seemed replaced by a big fire burning in the middle of a clearing. The yellow light danced against buildings of some sort, against moving figures and faces. There was the distinct smell of animal fat, horses, other things she couldn't identify. The sound of people talking loudly—softly—loudly—whispering. Of dogs barking, horses snorting.

Someone untied her hands and pulled her off Blaize. Her legs buckled, and she fell to the ground. More loud voices. Someone picked her up and carried her a short way. She had the distinct sensation of being set down on soft furs, then covered with something rough and wooly. Dimly she saw firelight dancing against the roof. At first it looked like light from a campfire reflected against a wagon's canvas. No, it couldn't be a wagon, the walls were round. She rubbed her eyes, stinging from smoke. She wasn't sure what she was seeing.

If only she weren't so thirsty, her brain so numb, her impressions so confused. They seemed to be drifting around like wisps of smoke, up, around, up, around, up through that hole above her toward the moon, drifting with the clouds that came back and forth across the moon. So tired. Where was she? Impossible to reason it out. Gradually, slowly, her brain seemed to take refuge in a dark void, a silent void—a welcome void.

She wasn't alone when she woke up. Someone was sitting just inside an opening in the room where sunlight streamed in. The opening looked like a large tent flap tied back. She noticed that the walls in the round room seemed to be made of animal skins, some of them painted in bright colors. Pictures of buffalo, elk, deer. They were being hunted by warriors on ponies, bows raised, arrows flying.

The person near the opening came over when she sat up, an old woman, with long gray hair, tied in bunches with beaded cords. When she spoke, Sarah Pearl noticed several teeth were missing, and her words came out strangely. Not that those words meant anything, though. They were unrecognizable, strange, clipped sounds. The old woman handed Sarah Pearl a small, brown pottery cup and pointed first to the cup, then to her mouth. That, at least, was understandable. Sarah Pearl threw back the blanket, guardedly reached for the cup, and took a hesitant sip—could they be trying to poison her? But the cool, wetness of the drink was welcome and she eagerly drained the cup, regardless. It tasted like some kind of berries, sweet and sour at the same time. Her tongue and lips felt kind of furry afterwards, but she was grateful her overwhelming thirst had disappeared.

"Where am I?" Sarah Pearl asked, pointing first to herself, then around the walls. She suspected it wouldn't make much difference whatever the woman answered. Sure enough, except for the word Shakota, she couldn't understand the woman's answer, even if it was in response to the question. Giving up, she pointed to the cup, then to her mouth. She seemed to be still alive after that drink, maybe she could risk another. The woman nodded, went over to a large, earthen jar, and ladled out more of the juice into the cup.

As she handed it to Sarah Pearl, she repeated the word Shakota. That touched a memory chord. Now Sarah Pearl remembered overhearing something Randy, the buffalo hunter, had said about the Shakota village to the north. That must be the answer. That's for sure where she'd been taken. And this strange, round tent-like place was what they called a teepee. She'd heard about them from her teacher at school back in Four Corners.

What else had she heard about Indians? Frantically she searched her mind for any bits of information she'd acquired from school, her father, her friends. She remembered seeing a few hunters coming in to trade furs at Bergstrom's store back in Four Corners. They spoke and looked a little similar.

She now realized these Shakota had only been after the buffalo hunters' horses. And the hunters had been after the Shakotas' buffalo. The irony was, though, the Shakota had come away with the horses. But without the horses, the buffalo hunters had no means of taking the buffalo. That is, if they had survived. She couldn't be sure. She'd left Jake lying on the ground, bleeding, shot through the arm. Been through worse, he'd said. She hoped that was true and that he was all right. He'd been kind and tried to protect her. In some ways he'd reminded her of her father, especially his voice. Yes, if only he was all right . . . Yet she knew he'd be dependent upon a horse, and his horse had come to this Shakota village with her.

"Blaize?" she asked. "The horse? Where's the horse I came with?"

The woman only shrugged and shook her head.

"What are you going to do with me?"

The woman shook her head again and gestured out beyond the teepee. At this Sarah Pearl shivered, remembering what Jake had said about murder, torture, and that he'd rather shoot her than let her fall into Shakota hands. She shivered again and drew the woven blanket more closely around her.

At this the old woman pointed to Sarah Pearl, then to a pile of clothes over in one corner. She held up a kind of shirt made of soft, yellowish leather, with a fringe around both the bottom and long sleeves. *Looks like deerskin*, Sarah Pearl thought. There was a design in blue and white beads around the neck opening. What looked like matching leather britches lay underneath the shirt. Saying something, the old woman approached her, holding out the leather clothes. She reached over to draw back the blanket.

"No, no," exclaimed Sarah Pearl, snatching it back under her chin. How was she going to put on these Shakota clothes without revealing she was actually a girl? "No," she cried again, shaking her head.

The woman laughed, pointing first to herself, then to the clothes, then to Sarah Pearl. With a sigh she picked up the empty pottery cup, untied the door flap and went out, letting it fall shut behind her. She'd understood. At least she'd assumed that the boy was too shy to undress in front of her, a woman, even an old woman, and left him some privacy.

As soon as she'd left, Sarah Pearl faced a dilemma. Should she do as the woman asked? It was tempting. Her own clothes—the Kerber boys' shirt, overalls, and jacket—were by now damp, smelly, and uncomfortable. She didn't know what had happened to Mr. Kerber's straw hat. She vaguely remembered seeing one of the Shakota picking it up, although the events of last night were still blurry in her mind.

As for her feet—well, they were in bad shape from walking on rocks or through prairie grass which could cut like sharp knives. Those soft leather shoes lying next to the britches, decorated with the same blue and white beads as the shirt, looked inviting.

Maybe all this meant they weren't planning to kill her. Torture, maybe. Torture her all dressed up like a sacrifice. No, she'd never heard stories about that. They weren't going to kill her. At least not right away. The anxiety of waiting, waiting for their next move—that would kill her. The anxiety of waiting for them to find out she was a girl, not a boy. What then?

She wasn't sure why, after pulling off Michael's shirt and Tom's overalls, she carefully rolled them up and wedged them under some fur rugs in the far corner of the teepee. Something didn't want to let them go. Perhaps because they were her only connection with another time, another world. With Michael—with Sophie—yes, even with that Tom. She was sorry about losing Mr. Kerber's hat.

Carefully, cautiously, she slipped on the leather clothes which the woman had laid out for her. Fingering her mother's silver heart locket, it felt warm to the touch, as if signaling her mother's presence, her mother's heart. That was comforting.

She hoped the locket wouldn't be visible under the leather shirt. She'd vowed never to take it off.

The clothes fit, more or less. The britches were a little tight across her hips and bum, the shirt too big. But that was good, because in came down just below her knees and was loose enough to disguise her upper parts, her upper parts about which she'd been so proud to show off. You're a woman now, my Pearl, Papa had said. Blossoming into a fine figure, just like your mother. Won't be long before all the boys in Four Corners will come courting. Just now, however, that blossoming seemed to be a liability. She had to disguise it in boy's clothes for as long as possible.

As for the shoes—soft as butter and a welcome transformation from a series of uncomfortable foot coverings, beginning with her own cracked and shrunken button shoes, then Michael's damp boots which were miles too big and blistered her bare feet. Although these butter-like things were also too big, she was able to pull the leather thongs around the cuff fairly tight. At least they stayed on her feet well enough, in fact, seemed to mold to the shape of her foot, moving when her foot moved, yet tough enough on the soles to protect against rocks or even prairie grass. She reflected on how great it would be always to wear shoes like that!

A bright flash of sunlight distracted these thoughts as the old woman re-entered the tent. She looked closely at Sarah Pearl, muttered something with a shake of her head, then pointed outside. The message was clear enough. Sarah Pearl had no choice but to follow, her leather garments making soft whispering sounds as she walked, those buttery shoes cushioning each step.

The teepees formed a large circle around a stone fire ring. A fire was still burning despite the fact it was after mid-day. Pieces of meat roasted on several spits over the fire, so large they could only have been from buffalo. The strange smell made Sarah Pearl feel a little nauseated, maybe because she hadn't eaten in so long. In fact, she couldn't remember when it had last been. At every occasion over the last two days, it seemed like food had been snatched away, either because she couldn't stomach it, or because there hadn't been time to eat it. The last she could remember were those dried apples she'd taken from the Kerbers' wagon when she'd first started out on her own, or maybe that dried up biscuit. That dried eel the buffalo hunters had—she shuddered, recalling all too vividly the sight, the smell of it.

Within the circle of teepees, much was going on. Near her, two young women, with very small children running around, were pounding grain of some sort in a mortar. Near them others were doing something with a buffalo hide stretched out on a wooden frame. The women were dressed a lot like the old woman leading her, except they wore their hair differently and several of them had their long skirts hiked up and tied around the waist. It looked like they were wearing men's britches underneath. The combination struck Sarah Pearl as practical, even if somewhat odd. Each one stopped her work to stare at Sarah Pearl as she passed, some looking quite amazed. The children giggled shyly at first, taking shelter behind their mothers, then slowly following her at a distance.

There was something very strange going on here. At first Sarah Pearl could not figure out what. Then the truth dawned. It wasn't only that village seemed empty except for women and children. Odder than that was the fact that all the children seemed so young—not much older than Sophie. There were none older, none her own age. What had happened to the others? More frightening was what this might mean for her.

She and the old woman were now passing by what seemed to be the main entrance to the village. At least it was marked by a pair of decorated posts, and the ground revealed a large number of hoof prints. Just outside the entrance was a corral, but there were only a few ponies and several horses moving around restlessly inside. No doubt those were the horses belonging to the buffalo hunters and included Blaize. It seemed weird, though. No older children, no men were in sight. Where were they?

No point in asking the old woman, who was urging her on by grasping her arm painfully and poking at her back. Obviously their destination was that large teepee on the other side of the circle, with two crossed spears stuck in the ground outside the door flap. Nor was it hard to guess this belonged to someone important.

The woman shouted something as she pulled up the flap, and they entered. Inside, two men were sitting cross-legged before a small fire in the center. A tall, young woman, dressed in a long deer-skin dress with a sort of feather cape around her shoulders, stood just behind them. Her hair hung down in two long braids, interwoven with colorful beaded bands, and a wide beaded band was over her forehead. She did not look up as Sarah Pearl entered the tent, but rather stared at the ground, clasping her hands nervously in front of her, holding, at the same time, a long, dark gray and white-tipped feather.

One of the men she recognized from the attack on the buffalo hunters—the one with the black and white feathers cascading down over his shoulders. The other was an older man, wearing what looked like a buffalo head with large horns and holes where the eyes once were. Parts of the buffalo's pelt came down over his shoulders and arms.

To her amazement, Mr. Kerber's straw hat was stuck on one of the horns, pierced right through the top, dangling and twirling around at a sharp angle. It looked so ridiculous she couldn't help bursting into uncontrolled laughter. It was as if suddenly her fear and tension had to find an outlet, to explode in a release of emotion, however inappropriate under the circumstances A painful jab in her right arm from the old woman immediately reminded her of how inappropriate it was, and Sarah Pearl swallowed hard several times to stifle any more outbursts.

Trying not to stare at the straw hat, she lowered her eyes and concentrated on the man's sleeveless vest, black-dyed leather decorated in red, blue, and black beads worked in between pieces of bone and quills. From his looks, Sarah Pearl assumed he must be the Shakota chief. Clearly she'd been brought before him to have her fate decided. It was almost like some old story, some ancient fairy tale. It couldn't be happening, no, not happening to her. It seemed as unreal as the ridiculous sight of Mr. Kerber's straw hat stuck on a buffalo horn. Her lungs were about to erupt again with choked-back laughter at the sight, and it was only by sheer will-power that she finally was able to bring it under control. That, and the thought of another painful jab from the old woman.

The old woman, however, was now leaving the tent, and the two men were engaged in some kind of dialogue. There was an obvious exchange of questions and answers, with a nodding of heads, gestures in her direction. Finally the chief beckoned to the woman standing behind him. She came to sit on the ground next to Sarah Pearl, and there followed a series of words with more gestures in Sarah Pearl's direction between the woman and the chief.

The woman nodded now and then at what the chief was saying. There was a pause between phrases while she looked off into the distance, stroking her cheek with the feather. At last the chief stopped speaking and the woman bowed her head for what seemed a very long minute.

Then, looking up at Sarah Pearl, she began hesitantly, "Buffalo Thunder ask—he say—ask—you—"

"Walahata!" The chief interrupted to say something in an angry tone.

"Ask me to speak—to speak—" she paused.

"You can speak my language?" Sarah Pearl asked in surprise. Amazement was more like it. It was a very different kind of amazement than seeing Mr. Kerber's hat dangling from a buffalo horn. Amazed relief was more like it.

"Not know many words. Forgotten. My name Walahata—mean Murmuring Water."

"But how do you—" She stopped at a stony look from the chief.

"Buffalo Thunder ask your name."

Sarah Pearl had to think fast. How about the one she'd used with the Buffalo Hunters? "William," she finally answered. Her father was still with her, perhaps his spirit would protect her.

The woman smiled faintly. "Not far like mine. I call you Will-hata-nam."

"What does that mean?"

"It mean Strong Waters. My name mean Murmuring Water."

How weird, Sarah Pearl thought, remembering the rushing currents of the James River where she'd nearly drowned. "How did you—" she wanted to ask how the woman knew that. She'd heard they had a way of knowing strange things, things known but not seen, perhaps, even, some contact with the spirit world. She shivered at this scary thought. "What happened—" she started again.

But Walahata raised her hand for silence. She paused, frowned, as if searching for words.

During that pause, Sarah Pearl took a closer look. Walahata seemed not quite like other Shakota she'd seen so far. Her long, braided hair wasn't totally black, but in amongst the beaded bands showed copper-like streaks. Her eyes were different, too—not exactly dark, but had a sort of greenish haze. It was hard to tell exactly, though, because she looked more often not at Sarah Pearl but rather at the chief or at the ground.

Who was this woman? Was it possible, she wondered, that she wasn't of the Shakota? She'd heard stories, strange stories about settlers who'd lost their children on the trails. Sometimes from attacks, sometimes from just wandering off. A whole host of possibilities raced through her mind, some of them, as they related to herself, frightening. "Who are you, really?" she blurted out, without considering whether this was appropriate or not under the circumstances. "Were you once with some of the settlers?"

The chief interrupted again sternly, at which Walahata shook her head. "Cannot say. Long time. Long, long time when—" She broke off, then pointed to Sarah Pearl. "You talk now. Chief say speak of Will-hata-nam."

By now, as a result of that first encounter with the Buffalo Hunters, Sarah Pearl had her answers fairly well rehearsed. "A while back I fell out of a wagon and lost my family."

"Not hunt buffalo with hunters?"

"No. Not hunting. Only with them."

"Why with them?" Walahata looked puzzled.

" Their cook."

"Ah," Walahata answered, and translated this for the chief and the man sitting beside him. At this the chief broke into loud laughter, slapping his knee and pointing to Sarah Pearl. There then followed a brief exchange between the two men, with instructions to Walahata.

"Chief Buffalo Thunder," she said, "laugh you do woman's work. He want teach you ways of Shakota braves. He find his son, Red Hawk. Red Hawk take you out when come back from hunt. Ride pony, shoot."

Sarah Pearl's alarm at this was hard to conceal. She'd never expected how far her boy's disguise might lead. It was, in fact, getting out of control. In fact, it looked like it was entering dangerous waters. Again, she couldn't put down memories of the James River. And then that strange coincidence, the Shakota meaning of her name. On the other hand, she reasoned, maybe there was some hope, consolation even, in what the chief had just said. They implied she wasn't going to be tortured or sacrificed. Not yet, at least. Not until they found out the truth.

Her face must have reflected her alarm, for Walahata said in a more consoling tone, "Red Hawk brave warrior, teach you much. Not hurt if do wrong. Teach do better." She stood up. "Now Buffalo Thunder say take back to teepee of Run Swift. Eat food. Wait for Red Hawk come back from buffalo hunt."

As they walked back to the old woman's teepee, Walahata seemed to sense Sarah Pearl's anxiety. "Do well. No punish. Willhata-nam become good brave. Good Shakota. Like Walahata."

"What do you mean? Do you mean you were—" How to pursue the subject of this woman's past without bringing back the pain she obviously felt? It seemed likely she'd been adopted into this Indian band some time ago. Yet the fact that she still remembered some English—or rather a kind of English—

seemed to suggest it hadn't been at too early an age. At last, though, curiosity got the better of her. Sarah Pearl had to find out what this woman remembered and where she might have come from. "How do you come to be—" she started to ask.

But Walahata interrupted her. "No talk," she insisted, shaking her head. "Forget much. Must forget." For a moment they walked in silence, followed by five or six curious young children. "Buffalo Thunder," she finally began, "want you Shakota. Not long time back, attack come from Black Wing warriors. Black Wing peoples take Shakota children to mountains. Lose many children. Now Buffalo Thunder need children, more sons. You not small child, but want."

Now it was becoming clear. Her fate was to be a replacement for a lost Shakota child. "But I don't belong here," she wailed. "I want to go home. My father—"

"Father long way. Like—" she broke off and quickly changed the subject. "Tomorrow you go hunt with Red Hawk, other men. You see. Now you go to teepee of Run Swift. She wait."

That seemed to signal that there were to be no more words between them. In silence, Sarah Pearl walked beside Walahata around the great bonfire toward the other end of the village, each step claiming her more and more a Shakota. Each step edging her more and more toward the inevitable disaster the truth of her identity would bring.

Could she make a break for it and run? An instant of hope! No, the reality was she wouldn't get very far. An alarm would go up, that brave in the chief's teepee would jump on one of the ponies over there in the corral and chase her down in seconds flat. Or she'd be shot in the back by his arrow. No, no way out of this unbelievable mess which she—or maybe just a series of circumstances—had created. A moment's reflection assured her that she had started them. She, Sarah Pearl Lundgren, in search of her father.

She glanced over at the corral as she passed. Among the several ponies moving restlessly around in that fenced-in space she spotted Blaize, Jake's horse, the white marking down his forehead easy to identify. One other horse she recognized as Sam's. Evidently the Shakota hadn't taken them all out on today's hunt. Could Blaize outrun a Shakota pony? Probably not. Even Jake and Randy thought the old horse unreliable. The plan she was slowly forming in her mind, however, would not go away. A risky plan, an insane plan.

The old woman named Run Swift welcomed Sarah Pearl back into her teepee with another cup of the berry-like drink. She motioned her to sit down on the fur rugs in one corner, said something, presented her with a kind of dark sausage on a woven straw mat, then left. Her last words clearly implied a warning.

Sarah Pearl looked around as she cautiously munched the sausage piece. It was very salty, but definitely an improvement over dried eel. The teepee was darker inside, now that the flap was down and the sun lower in the west. Still, she could tell that the animal skin walls were fastened securely all around the base with wooden stakes, leaving the door flap the only way out. And out there were many people, their numbers growing with the noisy return of the Shakota hunting party.

It seemed hopeless. Her survival was going to depend upon her success as a Shakota brave. The next thing would be wanting her to marry a Shakota girl. She could never get out of that one. Nature had its limits.

Suddenly the door flap was thrown back and Walahata entered. "I come, she announced, "with son of Buffalo Thunder."

A tall young man followed her in. He wore a bright red cloth twisted around his head, two quail feathers attached to the knot in back, leather britches like the ones given to Sarah Pearl, but was naked to the waist. His body gleamed with sweat from the recent ride. He sat down cross-legged on the floor close to the teepee entrance, while Walahata remained standing.

"Red Hawk say welcome." He nodded in Sarah Pearl's direction, and, not knowing quite how to respond, she nodded back. "Red Hawk say his father want you as son also. You now brothers."

This was the last thing Sarah Pearl expected. To pass as a boy was one thing. To become a brother was something else.

"Red Wing give gift to brother." She and the Shakota exchanged a few words in a low tone. After this, he rose and walked over to Sarah Pearl, drawing a long hunting knife with a carved horn handle out of his belt as he did so.

She drew back in terror. What did this mean? An instant sacrifice? Before she could do anything, Walahata came over and seized her arm. Pulling back the deerskin sleeve, she held tightly onto Sarah Pearl's wrist. Red Wing, with a kind of chant, slashed a small incision in her forearm, did the same to his own, and pressed the two bleeding wounds together.

"Now you share same blood," said Walahata. "Brothers." She smiled a little. "Now Walahata your sister. I marry Red Wing next new moon." They both stood up and prepared to leave the teepee. "Buffalo Thunder father to you, me, Red Hawk. Chief send gift." With that she unfolded a red and black blanket she'd been carrying. Sarah Pearl gasped in surprise. Inside was Mr. Kerber's old straw hat, with the gaping hole in the crown made by the chief's buffalo horn headdress. "Gift bring gift, no?"

Red Hawk laid his ornate hunting knife on the ground in front of Sarah Pearl with a gesture that looked like touching his hand to his heart, then opening up his palm to the sky. He waited, as if expecting something.

A gift? What could she offer him? The Kerbers' clothes? Hardly. Then she remembered the Kerbers' kitchen knife, which she stuck in the overalls' pocket. She scrambled down under the rugs in the corner for the clothes, found the knife, brought it out, and handed it to Red Hawk.

He stared at it, his astonishment quickly turning to contempt. He threw the knife down so hard that it penetrated a full three inches into the ground beside his own hunting knife. Sarah Pearl did not need Walahta's translation to tell her he thought this gift insulting to a warrior.

Something else, then? But she didn't have anything else. Suddenly she thought of Jake, how he'd handed her a small leather pouch when he told her to run and hide from the Shakota. It was still jammed down into the front pocket of her overalls. She drew it out and handed it to Red Hawk. She'd never had time to see what was in the pouch. She only hoped that, whatever it was, would be acceptable.

Red Hawk gave a murmur of pleasure as he pulled open the drawstrings and took out a silver dollar, an eagle engraved on one side. He smiled and bowed his head slightly at Sarah Pearl. It was acceptable.

But Walahata—she was looking expectant. There had to be something to offer, but there was nothing more. No, perhaps . . . She felt compassion for this woman, for all she must have been through. She had lost both father and mother, perhaps had few memories of them. Hadn't she once thought memories were a great gift? Perhaps in Walahata's case, they were more a curse.

The next moment Sarah Pearl found her hands unclasping the silver locket around her neck, drawing the chain out of her leather shirt, handing it to Walahata. Her mother's locket, her mother's picture, her mother's heart.

"Oh, Will-hata-nam!" she exclaimed. "One—long ago . . ." She pressed her hand over it as she held it to her heart, then to her lips. Her face contorted, as if tears and emotions were being held back through enormous efforts.

Now Sarah Pearl was fighting back tears. Yes, one—long ago. How strange to be connected here and now in this way. Like the rushing waters of her new name. This here and now. This Shakota family. Walahata's distant, unknown family. Her family. The Kerber family.

As Run Swift settled her down for the night, Sarah Pearl's brain raced around and around in her head. She was tempted to stay. She had unexpectedly formed a strong bond with Walahata, soon to be her sister. But no, she couldn't stay. Escape was necessary. Sooner or later they would find out the truth. Once Buffalo Thunder discovered he had a daughter, not a son named Will-hata-nam—well, that would be the end of her for sure. She suspected the old chief would take more seriously her lies about her identity than the fact she could not become his warrior son. A fleeting thought, a wild thought—take Walahata with her?

After hours of sleeplessness, Sarah Pearl gradually became aware that the village had grown quiet. In the distance a few dogs barked half-heartedly, answered more seriously by some wolves farther away. Soft footsteps passing occasionally by the teepee confirmed someone out there on guard duty. Inside the teepee, however, Run Swift's snores implied she was more or less unguarded.

Yet how to get out? The stinging sensation on her forearm reminded her of Red Hawk's hunting knife. And that knife reminded her that, when he'd thrown down her offered Kerbers' kitchen knife in disgust, it had cut right through the floor covering. Why not try the wall with Red Hawk's knife—longer, sharper, better. If she could just slit open a hole big enough in the back to crawl through—quietly, on course. She dare not wake up Run Swift. If Run Swift were true to her name, she'd be running right after her, waking up the whole village. Even if she'd acquired that name when she was still young, she was a very determined-looking woman. Yet it was worth a try. She had little to lose—well, only her life, actually.

For nearly an hour she cautiously cut through the skin of the back wall very close to the ground. She bunched up the fur rug in front of her, in case Run Swift woke up and saw what she was doing. At last the opening seemed just big enough to slip through, providing it was one arm or one leg at a time, then at last her whole body.

But what to do about the gifts? Her Shakota clothes? Her conscience getting the better of her, she carefully and slowly removed them. It wouldn't be right to keep them. With great reluctance she pulled out from under the fur rugs where she'd hidden them Michael Kerber's gray flannel shirt and Tom's smelly overalls and jacket. Strange, how they seemed to change her into someone else. Not the Sarah Pearl she once knew. And not the Sarah Pearl of the Kerbers' wagon, either. They felt rough and foreign upon her body, not at all as comfortable as the Shakota clothes.

Once dressed, she picked up Mr. Kerber's straw hat for good measure and held it tightly under her arm. Creeping on her hands and knees across the teepee floor to recover the old kitchen knife—it might be useful later, she laid Red Hawk's beautiful hunting knife back down exactly where he'd placed it. It was a gift she could not, in all conscience, keep. The power of her gift of the locket to Walahata, the emotion and pleasure she read in the woman's eyes, was gift enough. And now Walahata—could she find her, persuade her to escape with her?

It seemed the moment to try. Silently, cautiously, she pulled apart the slash in the teepee wall and crawled through. Once outside, a gentle breeze ruffled her short, cropped hair, the cold, dewy grass was a shock to her bare feet. She jammed on the old straw hat, thankful that it had shrunk enough in the rain that first night to fit snuggly. She eyed the clouds racing across the moon. Like the night before, the moon shone between gaps in the clouds, revealing alternating illumination and shadow.

She looked around the village circle to teepees. A shadow moved on the far side. A dog barked close by. Which teepee was Walahata's? Her heart sank as she realized there was no way of knowing. The wrong choice, the wrong move would ruin everything. Besides, what if she did find Walahata and she refused to leave with her? Would she give her away? No, with a sense of overwhelming sadness, she'd have to try to escape alone.

Crawling along the ground behind the nearest teepees, Sarah Pearl slowly snaked her way toward the corral. At the slightest sound or movement, she lay still until she thought it safe to move forward. In the corral was Blaize. Slipping him out somehow was the only way she'd be able to get far enough away before dawn and, hopefully, before they discovered her missing. And then she'd find a trail somewhere and head east. East to Four Corners, and Four Corners to home. Home to where she'd last seen her father. From there? She'd work that out later, no time now.

At last she reached the log stakes forming the corral fence and waited until the moon hid behind racing clouds. In that instant she slipped through a narrow gap. She froze as several ponies whinnied softly, then moved cautiously through them once they quieted down. Suddenly the moon emerged and bathed everything in ghostly light. And in that light stood Blaize at the corral gate, as if waiting for her.

With a gasp, Sarah Pearl saw that the moonlight revealed something else. Next to Blaize stood another horse. Not Sam's, not Randy's. A different horse. A large horse with three white legs and one brown. No, no, it couldn't be! But it was. It was Boone—Boone! The Kerbers' one horse, the one Tom usually rode! Boone seemed to recognize her. He nuzzled her shoulder with a soft whinny. But what was Boone doing here?

Something must have happened to the Kerbers, to Tom—to Michael and the others. It was clear they were not in this Shakota village. Were they dead?

This was a mystery she had no way to solve without questioning Walahata. And there was no way to do that now. No turning back. Escape must be immediate, or else—

Nevertheless, she couldn't stop wondering about the Kerbers and how their horse came to this Shakota village. Possibly they'd been captured somehow, perhaps killed, their graves nearby—Mrs. Kerber's, Tom's, Sophie's, Michael's, all in a row. The thought of Michael's grave created a wave of unexpected emotion in her heart, her brain. She couldn't explain it. What had happened? Were her fears out of real concern? That was a question she was half-afraid to answer. Even if she did answer the question honestly, she couldn't do anything about it. Did she even want to find him—or them, for that matter?

But best not pursue those thoughts. There was no time. Her own life was in danger. Right now, she must focus only on getting a horse silently and unseen out the corral gate. And she would not take old, tired Blaize. She would take Boone.

To her relief, Boone came out without hesitating, as if as eager to escape as she. Although he had no saddle, Sarah Pearl was grateful he still wore his bridle and bit. She managed to fasten shut the corral gate before Blaize followed him out, all too willing, it seemed, to escape with her. No, on second thought. Let Blaize out, too. Then if she were followed, there'd be the confusion of two trails and the question of which one to follow. At least that was something she'd heard somebody say—make a false trail to confuse your pursuers. Perhaps he might even make his way to Jake, somewhere. A long shot, a wild hope, even were he still alive. But weren't miracles possible?

Stepping up on a nearby tree stump, she threw her right leg over Boone's back and pulled herself all the way up by hanging onto his mane. She'd once boasted to Michael she could ride bareback. Here was the test. Pressing her legs against the horse's sides, she leaned forward and whispered, "Go, Boone, go Daniel Boone! Softly as you can up to the edge of those trees. No noise, no noise."

Glancing behind her back toward the village, all seemed quiet except for a dog barking and a bit of restlessness in the corral. Maybe the Shakota were used to that, and wouldn't think it unusual. Blaize had already burst through the gate and disappeared into the darkness in another direction. "Find Jake," Sarah Pearl whispered after him. "Oh, please find him."

Holding Boone back to a mere walk, she reached the first stand of pines. Another break in the clouds revealed an opening between the next group, and then the next. The thickness of the trees and the unevenness of the ground would make it hazardous, but she had to risk it.

"Fly, now, Boone," she hissed in his ear. "Fly like the wind wherever the way takes us." She loosened the horse's reins and dug both heels into his flanks as they entered the first dark corridor among the trees. "Let's hope that way is home."

Chapter 7

SONG OF THE WOLVES

AHOOO! Rooo! Ahoooo! All night long, wolves howling, shrieking, singing their spine-chilling songs. A whole chorus, answering each other from one side of the forest to another, from one hilltop to another, circling in for the kill. Several times Sarah Pearl wondered whether it might be Shakota following her and signaling to each other. If so, it wouldn't be long before they circled in on her. Something was following her, betrayed by a twig snapping, the swosh of branches, a voice wordless, something breathing.

How long this night seemed! Only when the moon came out from behind the clouds was it safe to go faster along what looked like a narrow track through the forest. But once the moon disappeared, she had to rein Boone in to keep from losing her way or getting hit by low hanging branches. Already she'd been whacked a few times, with branches wet with dew. It didn't help her Kerber-borrowed clothes, damp and stinking. She'd had to take off Mr. Kerber's straw hat and tuck it under her left thigh to keep from losing it.

And with the ground often uneven, there was always a danger of Boone's falling into a hole and breaking a leg. Then where would they be? She be? You had to shoot a horse when it broke its leg.

No, it wouldn't be long before the Shakota discovered the right trail and tracked them down. With their keen hunting and tracking senses, they'd spot it a mile off. What good would her newly acquired status as chief Buffalo Thunder's adopted son, Will-hata-nam be? For sure, totally ignored, or worse, work against her. She'd be regarded as betraying them. Then where would he—no, she meant she—be? You had to do away with a person who lied like that.

At last the night seemed to be ending. She was aware of the faint promise of pale sky growing behind silhouetted branches overhead. It was reassuring to hear the rising twitter of morning birds and the wolves growing fainter. Coming to a hill where the trees thinned, she cautiously rode Boone up toward the top.

"Careful, boy," she hung on close to his mane and whispered into his ear. "Let's see if we can tell what direction we're going. We should be heading east, toward where the sun's about to come up. That'll put the Shakota village behind us. Very far behind us, let's hope! That is, if we haven't been riding around in circles!" It occurred to her this might be a possibility.

Urging Boone to the crest of the hill, she waited nervously for the first signs of sunrise. "Watch now. When the sun comes up, it'll break through somewhere along that low bank of clouds. That'll be east and show us the way home!"

But something was wrong, very wrong. The sun wasn't coming up. It was getting darker, not lighter. Black clouds were spreading across the sky and the rumble of distant thunder signaled a storm. The early morning breeze had turned into a sharp, cold wind. Boone whinnied nervously.

"Better get down off this hill, Boone." The hill was steeper going down and Sarah Pearl almost pitched off headlong into the brush. About halfway down she gasped in surprise.

There—directly in front of her—was what looked like an old wagon trail! Wheel ruts deep into the sod showed that wagons had passed that way, although by the looks of the grass growing over them it was sometime ago. It must lead to somewhere. But which way should she go? Left or right? Without the sun's help, she couldn't tell which way was east.

Surely, though, either way she'd meet settlers passing in their wagons. Then she'd know. Then she'd have some protection. Something to eat. Maybe even some word of home—Four Corners—her father. Surely settlers moving west would come through there, might have heard of her father, William Lundgren, and of their old homestead east of town.

The rain held off, although the air was turning colder and the wind stronger. Sarah Pearl pulled up the collar of Tom's jacket closer around her neck and shivered. Not that Mr. Kerber's straw hat was much help, especially with that big hole from being stuck through a horn on Chief Buffalo Thunder's headdress. She wished she'd at least kept those soft leather shoes from Running Swift's teepee. Her bare feet were freezing. To add to her problems, Boone was tiring. Foamy lather dripped from his muzzle and he kept stumbling.

"All right, Boone. We'll rest a bit." She looked anxiously down the trail in both directions. On the other side of the trail and several yards to the left there appeared to be a large formation of big rocks. "Well, Boone," she commented, "looks like we're in luck. See that spring coming down through a couple of rocks?"

She slid off Boone's back, climbed a ways up the formation, and lay flat on her stomach to drink from the water trickling down. It was cold. It was life-giving.

Feeling somewhat better, Sarah Pearl decided to let Boone graze on the grassy trail a little longer. He was probably too tired to wander far. She climbed farther up the rock formation to get a better view of the trail, trying to avoid the sharp edges of the dark, reddish rocks. Now there was a clearer view of the trail in both directions.

But which direction should she take? Which way was east? With the sky still so heavily overcast, it was impossible to tell.

At that moment she remembered something she'd learned from Tom Kerber. Maybe that boy was good for something after all. He'd once pointed out that the wind across the prairies usually came from the west or southwest. That's was why we ain't making good time, he'd said. Always heading into the wind, always fighting it.

So—surely if the wind she was feeling now, standing on top of this rock formation, was on her back, all she had to do was keep it that way. Then she'd be turning left onto the trail— to the east—toward home!

Looking long and hard toward the horizon, she became aware of black speck against the dark yellow-green of prairie grass. Bit by bit that speck grew larger. From time to time it came into sharper focus against a background of red or yellow rocks.

Fear or relief? Her knees felt weak, her palms sweaty, and her heart beat wildly. Shakota, coming after her? Or a wagon load of settlers?

Quickly she scrambled down the rocks, snatched up Boone's reins, and led him around behind the rocks to a sort of overhanging ledge. It was more or less screened from the trail by some scrub pine. "Boone, if ever you needed to keep quiet, if ever you needed not to whinny at anything—anything on earth—this is the time. I'm going to tie you to this tree. Don't move—not a single hoof, while I try to figure out what's coming down that trail. But be ready to take off. We may have to." She knew they'd have little chance of out-distancing Shakota on fast ponies, but she had to try. Her life depended on it.

Keeping as much out of sight as possible, she climbed up the far side of the rock pile. She crouched down as low as she could and watched the black speck in the distance grow bigger and bigger. It seemed now less than a mile off. At that moment a spattering of raindrops hit her face and a sheet of rain swept across the prairie. In the distance the black speck stopped moving.

What was happening to it? She still couldn't make out what it was. Riders on horses or ponies? A wagon? The black speck began to move again. Slowly at first, then faster.

The next moment Sarah Pearl could identify it. A wagon and team! The first of a wagon train? Maybe the Johnson wagon train? Looking more closely, she realized it was a single wagon. The discovery was disappointing, but a relief nonetheless. She'd take Boone and meet them. Maybe there'd be a girl about her size who'd loan her some decent clothes. What a great thing it would, just getting out of this Kerber stuff!

Untying Boone, she slid up to his back and urged him into a gallop toward the wagon, now jolting slowly along the trail. The rain drove into her face, but she scarcely noticed it.

Now only about a hundred yards away, the wagon stopped a second time. Someone jumped out and started running towards her, shouting. Rushing right at her, Sarah Pearl had no choice but to rein in Boone sharply to the right, causing him to rear. Slipping on the wet grass and falling to the ground, nearly under Boone's hooves, was—Sophie Kerber.

And behind Sophie Kerber there came an ox team and wagon. "Whoa, whoa!" came a sharp command, and the wagon came to a halt.

"Tom?" a voice called out through the rain. "Tom—is-ss that you? Oh, is-ss it you?"

"No, Maw, wait—" Michael's voice. Sarah Pearl could recognize it anywhere. The same for Mrs. Kerber with her snake-like hisses.

Mrs. Kerber jumped down and rushed towards Sarah Pearl. "Oh, Tom—my boy—"

In an instant, Sarah Pearl grasped the reality of it all. And the reality was beyond words, the last possible thing in the whole world she expected—this meeting up with the Kerber wagon. In the middle of nowhere. Beyond belief! Of all the trails—east, west, north, south—this had to be the one Boone had stumbled upon.

Mrs. Kerber fell to the ground alongside Sophie and seized Sarah Pearl's leg, hugging it and sobbing uncontrollably. "Oh, Tom—Tom—you're back!" With that she looked up, then struggled to her feet and took a sudden step backward, her face contorted in horror. "You're not Tom. Oh—oh—not my Tom!"

"Sophie—Maw—get—come back—get back into the wagon, out of the rain." Michael's voiced sounded strange. "Can't you see it's not Tom? It's only that—that girl! And—and on our horse, Boone!"

"Mamie," Sophie cried between sobs, "Sawah wear Tom jacket. Pappie hat!"

Sarah Pearl was speechless. What was going on? Whether from shock or the cold, or the driving rain, she saw her hands begin to shake and couldn't control her teeth from chattering. It was as if she were frozen in place on Boone, and Boone's hooves were nailed with his shoes to the ground.

"Maw," Michael repeated, "it's not our Tom, only Tom's clothes. Come on, bring Sophie into the wagon out of the rain."

Mrs. Kerber in a state of shock slowly picked up Sophie. Michael reached down to help her up onto the driving bench, from where she climbed through the canvas opening into the rear of the wagon.

"You stay back there with Sophie, Maw," Michael turned to shout. "It looks like there's some kind of shelter—some rocks with a kind of overhang. We'll pull in there." He threw a furtive glance in Sarah Pearl's direction, started to say something, but changed his mind. Instead he pulled his hat down farther over his eyes, hunched his shoulders, and snapped his whip at the oxen. Slowly the team strained the wagon forward. Sophie was wailing back in the wagon, interspersed with Mrs. Kerber's hissing consolations.

Was this really happening? It seemed incredible to Sarah Pearl, meeting the Kerbers at this point in the trail, still moving west. Was it possible that the Shakota village was farther to the east than she'd thought? That during last night she'd gotten confused about directions? Not surprising, considering her forced movements over the past few days. First with the buffalo hunters and then with the Shakota.

Now there was a choice, although one more difficult to make than ever. She could rejoin this family to whom she didn't belong. Or, she could urge Boone forward and slip past them, so continuing east down the wagon trail as she'd originally planned.

It occurred to her, however, that to continue east on her own she might encounter the Shakota, pursuing her on their ponies. She was hungry and tired. Wearing filthy boy's clothes, Kerber clothes. Her feet were freezing cold. Boone was done in. Besides, she'd have to ride on past them down the trail on their horse. And what had they said about losing Tom? What had happened to him? Had he and Boone been in that Shakota village, all along? Perhaps, in taking Boone, she'd actually prevented him from escaping. The more she considered the matter, the more impossible was either choice.

Worse, still, was the fact that, Tom Kerber, as pesky and obnoxious as he was, still reminded her of her lost little brother, Jason. The brother she had lost, truth be told. As well, Tom had, after all, rescued her once. On Boone. And for that matter, so had Michael. From the James River.

"No, Maw," she heard Michael shouting through the rain from the wagon's driving bench, "you and Sophie stop your carryings on. No, it's not Tom, but don't worry. We'll find him yet."

Now she was forced to rein Boone off the trail as the Kerber's wagon passed. "Follow us, Miss," Michael commanded rather icily. "That is, if you've a notion to."

Not that she had any notion to, but under the circumstances it seemed the better choice. So, reining Boone around, she reluctantly followed the slowly-moving Kerber wagon and team through the rain back west down the trail.

Within a few minutes they reached the rock formation with the spring. "See that ledge behind them rocks?" Michael shouted. "We'll wait there for the rain to let up."

There wasn't much shelter there, but it was mostly out of the rain. For Sarah Pearl it was a very awkward situation. It didn't escape her, though, it might also be awkward for the Kerbers. From over the tailgate at the back of the wagon, Sophie kept staring at her in awe. Mrs. Kerber, on the other hand, seemed distant and cool, sniffing between bouts of sobs. Michael, for once, seemed at a loss. "Maw, tighten them pucker strings, will you," was all he said.

Finally she couldn't stand the tension, his avoidance, the unspoken words any longer. "Michael," she said, hesitantly joining him where the oxen were drinking from a large puddle, "what happened to Tom? Can you tell me? I need to know."

"Tom? Oh, Tom. Well, you see. It was—" he stopped, concentrating on the oxen.

"Well?"

"It was like this—it was . . ." He paused, hesitant, busying himself tightening up the harnesses, checking the spokes of the wheels. After a few moments, he drew up his shoulders and faced her squarely as if he'd made up his mind about something.

"It was like this. Guess you have a right to know, 'cause it concerns you." She wasn't sure whether his eyes reflected hate or hostility or both. She turned away, preparing herself for the worst.

"You disappeared," he began.

"I needed to—needed to—" She couldn't explain.

"Well, you disappeared. No way of knowing what happened. Stopped at the next watering hole, you were gone. Plumb gone, disappeared. Tom had an idea 'bout that."

"Tom?"

"Kept insisting you'd fallen out. Kept saying, 'She fell out, like she done before.'"

"Tom said that?"

"Thought you probably hurt yourself, maybe even got knocked out, couldn't yell or anything. So he wanted to ride back to find you, just like he did before." He paused. "I didn't know 'bout that. Tom never told me—or Maw."

"He rode back on Boone?"

"Maw kept on saying too risky, no telling how far back you were. Said you were sure to be picked up by the next wagon train coming through." He paused again. "Maw felt about you—well, you know she didn't—" He broke off.

Michael didn't have to say it. Sarah Pearl knew Mrs. Kerber disliked her and felt she wasn't as much help on this trek as she'd expected. She was sure Mrs. Kerber only thought of her as a nuisance, another mouth to feed. And, if it came to that, resented the fact that Papa had disappeared and left her that responsibility. Feeling hurt by Michael's words, nevertheless, she was anxious to hear more about what had happened to Tom. "You mean, Tom rode back to find me anyway?"

"Maw protesting the whole time. We went kind of slow like for a few miles, hoping he'd catch up. But he didn't. Stopped the wagon right there at that watering home for the night, hoping he'd find his way back." He paused, looked down as if embarrassed. "I was hoping he'd come back with you."

"With me? You wanted me back?" This was hard to believe, coming from Michael.

He didn't answer. Instead, he looked thoughtfully up at the sky. "Rain's let up. Sky clearing. Best move on."

"What could have happened to him, then?" Sarah Pearl persisted, taking hold of his arm. She had to talk about it, even if Michael seemed unwilling. Her mind teemed with possibilities. Most of them concerned the Shakota village.

"You best tell me what you know—you're the one riding Boone. Where'd you find him?"

"Found him in a corral in a Shakota village."

"Tom was there, then?" he asked eagerly. "You saw him?"

"No," she answered slowly, giving herself time to think. "I didn't see him. There was no sign of him there, or anything to show he'd ever been there. You know, those Shakota value horses over their ponies. They'll trade for them, or . . . or . . ." She didn't want to describe the alternatives, let alone how she and Blaize were captured and led away into the night.

"You were in their village?" Michael stared at her in disbelief. "How'd that happen? How'd they treat you?" Was he implying some concern for her?.

Just then Mrs. Kerber came over, leaning on her cane and holding Sophie by the hand. "Got the child changed into dry clothesss and calmed down a bit." Looking directly at Sarah Pearl, she added, "You'd bes-sst change. Laid out a few things-ss for you in the wagon." There was a long pause. "Tom's-ss things-ss. Reckon they'll fit, like they done before." She turned away with several decisive sniffs. "Boys-ss' things-ss. It'll take a while for your hair to grow out," in an acid tone, accompanied by more sniffs.

Mrs. Kerber immediately re-directed her attention to Sophie and Michael. "Now, Michael, we've got to move on. Find better shelter 'fore nightfall. Rain's-ss let up, looks-ss like. Don't know what we can eat tonight, though, with food running out and all."

With a sigh, she handed Sophie to Michael. "Hold on to her, not sure I can trust the girl. I've got to hitch up Boone to the back of the wagon. He ss-sure looks-ss the worst for wear." She gave a dark look in Sarah Pearl's direction.

Sarah Pearl knew she was being blamed for everything. "I'm sorry, ma'am, about Tom," she heard herself choking out. "Very sorry. All my fault."

But if she expected an answer, some degree of reassurance, she was disappointed. Neither Mrs. Kerber nor Michael said anything more. Rather, they busied themselves with the wagon, the horse, the oxen, Sophie.

"Get yourself into the wagon, Sarah, like Maw says," Michael said eventually, somewhat hesitantly, partially between his teeth. He quickly looked away. "Maw, you best come up here on the bench with Sophie and me. We should be on our way.

No telling what's coming behind us, what's out there. Wolves—heard them all last night, not too far off. Coyotes, too, maybe. And Shakota, for sure! Climb in back there and get on some dry clothes, Sarah."

Sarah—he had called her just Sarah. For the first time it wasn't Miss, or girl, or you, or implied stupid or too talkative or too difficult. It was not even Sarah Pearl. Sarah Pearl wondered what this meant, why the change, especially at this moment when she was being accused of Tom's loss and held guilty for a likely tragedy. It was puzzling, not to mention disturbing.

The wagon jolted forward as she fell back over the tailgate, once more finding herself on the wagon floor, resisting moving in the opposite direction she desired, but now too cold, hungry, and exhausted to care. No, that wasn't true. She did care about something.

Only one thought now filled her mind. She'd been responsible for the Kerbers' losing Tom. Even though she'd recovered their horse, that wasn't much consolation. Not only were they without Tom. From the looks of things, they were in an over-all bad situation—exhausted, without much food left. What kind of apology could she make? What compensation?

No, there was another thought, too. Michael—Michael Kerber, for the first time, had talked to her, openly and with some concern in his voice. And he had called her by name. Not once, but twice. And not by the name Sarah Pearl. Certainly not by her father's pet name, Pearl. He had called her simply, Sarah.

Chapter 8

THE HAUNTED CAVE

FOR the rest of that day the sun appeared, disappeared. Clouds formed, parted, formed again, grew darker and heavier as the hours passed. Strong winds veered from west to east, then shifted from northwest to north, bringing a sharp edge.

"Storm coming for sure," Michael was saying to his mother from the driving bench. Sarah, half-dozing lying wrapped in quilts in the back of the wagon, only heard a word now and then. At the word "storm," however, she paid better attention.

"Only to be expected this-ss time of the year. End of the ss-summer—heading into fall already."

"Surely no snow this early, though that north wind has the smell of it. Dunno know how we could—" He broke off, clearly worried. "By my calculations, there's still another fifty miles or so 'fore we reach Discovery and the claim. Another two, three days."

"Hopefully we won't run into ss-snow yet. Although I heard Mr. Johnson tell your Paw, way back when we ss-started with the Johnson train in Ohio, that ss-snow storms-ss can hit early this-ss far west in the Dakota territory."

"Don't seem quite cold enough yet for that storm ahead to bring snow. Just rain, and a lot of it, too. From the looks of it, prob'ly have to make camp early tonight."

Sarah, just getting warm and comfortable among the quilts

in dry clothes, was wide awake. It bothered her that the clothes were Tom's—a brown-and-green plaid shirt and denim overalls. But it was either that or her pink silk dress in the carpet bag in the chest, or—even worse, Mrs. Kerber's next best mourning outfit. Not that boys-ss' clothes are suitable, she'd heard Mrs. Kerber comment dryly to Michael, but I'm of the opinion, with her hair all chopped off like, anything else'd look wrong.

Sarah was relieved that Michael made no answer to this. She knew it hurt him to see her in Tom's things, a constant reminder of his loss. At least she was wearing her own, worn-out boots, which she'd left in the wagon before her escape. Unfortunately they felt more uncomfortable than before. Instinctively her hand felt for the silver locket around her neck, but suddenly she remembered she'd given it to Walahata. Somehow her feeling of loss was about equal to the joy she'd seen in Walahata's eyes when she'd accepted it. Yes, it had been the right thing to do.

Now, thinking once again of the Widow Kerber and when she'd given her Tom's clothes, it seemed she looked a little different. It was hard to describe. Mrs. Kerber looked older, thinner, grayer, paler, shorter and somehow less witch-like. She didn't hiss as much, it seemed to her, or else she'd simply gotten used to it. Try as she might to resist it, Sarah couldn't help but feel a twinge of pity for her, just as she'd felt for Walahata.

What had Michael been saying? Her mind went back to the conversation she'd just heard from the front of the wagon regarding the weather and making camp early that night. The howling wolves were bad enough, but far worse was the distinct impression that the Shakota were tracking them. She loosened the pucker string closing the canvas cover behind the driving bench and poked her head out. She needed to ask Michael something however reluctant he might be to answer.

"Michael, how far do you think we've come since I met you back there?"

"Oh, 'bout ten miles, I reckon. Been working Blue and Big Horn hard's I can. On their last legs—already worn out from this trek. Can't do much better'n this."

"Lucky if they las-sst 'til Discovery," Mrs. Kerber added. The worry and despair on her face was evident.

This alarmed Sarah even more and, with that, something else. It wasn't only the thought of her own danger from the Shakota. Failing—that was it. The Kerbers failing in their journey, so close to the end and especially after loosing Tom. She was surprised at feeling this way about Tom, about the Widow Kerber—about Michael, even. It was a little hard to understand. "You said a storm's coming up?" she heard herself saying, unwilling reveal what she'd just been thinking.

"Ss-see those leaden-gray clouds over there?" Mrs. Kerber pointed ahead. "Lightning flashes, and listen to that thunder. We're heading right into it—don't see how we can avoid it." She held Sophie more closely and turned to Michael. "Can't you get a bit more out of those beasts?"

"Doing my best, Maw."

Mrs. Kerber pointed to the canvas covering. "Sarah Pearl, see that all the canvas is tied down, everything in the back secure." Turning her back to Sarah and looking straight ahead, she muttered, "Can't risk anymore loss, can we?"

Suddenly a tremendous snap of lightening cracked the air all around them, followed by a clap of thunder ripping the whole sky apart. Then another—and another.

"Got to get out of this," Michael shouted. "Find shelter quick. Those clouds about to burst." He turned toward the back of the wagon. "Hang on, Sarah! But first, Maw—Sophie'll be safer back there—hand her back to Sarah. You may have to give me a hand with the team." Her own name! Michael had used it again!

"Sawah! Sawah!" Now Sophie was crying, frightened, clinging to her. Sarah wrapped a quilt around them both as they wedged themselves into a corner of the wagon just behind the driving bench. She cushioned them against it with the straw mattress and whatever else she could find, for the speed of the wagon was now creating such shocks and jolts that she feared they might be thrown from one side to another and their limbs broken. "Hush, hush, little Sophie," she tried to say soothingly. "We're snug and safe now."

It was clear they were anything but. As the wagon continued west down the trail, rushing right into the storm ahead, every inch of the wagon, inside and out, seemed to be shaking loose. Hanging on pegs along the wall, the clothes swayed wildly. Things shifted and rolled and bounced. The box with the knives, forks, and spoons spilled across the floor, clattering back and forth and made a curious symphony of metallic sounds.

In all of this confusion, Sarah's thoughts tried to focus on something else, something more reassuring, more comforting. Sarah. Michael was calling her not Miss, not Sarah Pearl, just simply Sarah. It sounded strange. Yet she liked it. She'd never been happy with her double name, relieved that Papa had always called her just Pearl—his precious pearl. And now in this new life, it seemed right. A comfort. Just right.

In another instant a torrent of rain hit the wagon heavily. Michael shouted to the oxen, despite the fact they seemed to be struggling as well as they could. "Can't see," he yelled to Mrs. Kerber above the noise, "can't see the trail."

"Shelter—find—no use—soon—" Mrs. Kerber was shouting back.

Sophie began to cry, with intermittent screams of fear after each thunderclap. Sarah worried about Boone, struggling to keep up with the wagon. Several times he reared and threatened to break loose from the rope tied to the rear axle. There was nothing she could do except hang onto Sophie tightly and try to keep both of them from being thrown around from one side of the wagon to the other, along with the knives, forks, spoons, and everything else.

"Up there ahead—" Michael was yelling against the wind and rain. "Got to make for it—cliff—maybe find—" His words were drowned out by the storm and Sophie's terrified screams.

Sarah closed her eyes and hung on. The next minute she felt the wagon lurching downward, the wheels hitting a few rocks or crunching down into holes. Michael was shouting at the oxen—"Hup, hup, haw! Haw!" She had a graphic image of their earlier descent down the bank of the James River. It seemed like the same thing was happening again, only without her help with the brakes, or Tom's help with the wheel chocks.

She couldn't help re-living that awful fear of plunging down out of control. Or the fear of being swept downstream with Sophie, helpless and gasping for air, until Michael pulled her out by her hair.

Her hair, her beautiful long braid—gone. In all the confusion and drama of the present head-long rush of the wagon into danger, fragments of thoughts raced through her mind. Her role as a boy, first as William-the-Buffalo-Hunter, then as Will-hata-nam. And it occurred to her that over the past many weeks, she'd become more than Sarah Pearl Lundgren of Four Corners. She'd lived through other lives, learned many, many things, until now she'd become—just Sarah, a very different Sarah. Perhaps that was a comfort, too. She wasn't quite sure.

"This'll do!" Michael shouted, with a "Whoa—whoooah boys," to the oxen. "Do just fine here 'til the storm stops."

Hearing this brought Sarah sharply back to the present situation. She realized the wagon had stopped. The rain seemed to have stopped, too, although it still drummed against the ground and swirled over the rocks. It took a moment to understand what had happened. Looking out over the wagon's tailgate, she saw they were standing just inside the entrance to a large cave. A curtain of water cascaded noisily down across the opening. Behind them were darkness and the faint sound of winds, moaning deep down in distant caverns. She couldn't decide which seemed more frightening, inside the cave or outside.

Michael stood in the cave entrance, looking out at the storm. "Not much sign it's letting up," he remarked. "Best rest a while, dry out. Looks like we'll be here for the night. Maw, you do what you can for some dry clothes, while I try to build a fire, warm us up a bit."

"Can I help?" Sarah asked.

He looked at her thoughtfully. "Like what?"

"Must be something," she ventured. "Like gathering up some wood for the fire."

"Here? In this cave?"

"Maybe there's something. I'll look around."

"Well, you do just that." Was that meant as a sneer? "Meantime, I've got a few sticks of dry kindling left in the wood box." He climbed up on the wagon tongue to pull out a long, hinged box under the driving seat. "And make sure Sophie don't wonder off again. Like last time."

That hurt. But by this time she'd come to realize that Michael probably didn't mean his words to hurt. He didn't have a way with words. He just didn't know how to handle difficult situations, her being one. Fortunately Sophie was in the wagon with her mother, so Sarah needn't worry on that account.

The front part of the cave was enormous, reaching up fifty feet or so, and in width swallowing up the entire wagon and team. As she looked around just inside the entrance, she discovered a few branches and some piles of dry leaves which had blown in. She drew back in horror gathering up the last pile of leaves when they revealed the bones of a skeleton, an old, rusty musket. She didn't stop to look closer.

Michael threw her leaves and twigs onto the small fire he'd started, but not without a suppressed look of surprise. His only remark, however, was, "We'll be needing more."

This time Sarah had to venture farther into the cave. She returned empty handed. "That's all I could find. It was too dark to look for more," she began apologetically, knowing his response would probably be something like, "told you so."

But to her surprise, he said, "If you'll wait a second, I'll light the kerosene lantern. It'll help and," he hesitated, "and you'll be safer. No telling what's farther on back there. Likely to be holes, tunnels, maybe. Hear that wind? From the sound of it, howling and moaning, seems like a mighty big cave, miles and miles, maybe." He managed a faint smile and a wink in her direction. "Bats, too."

That he would say this much—and in this way—was unexpected, although she hoped Michael didn't notice her shiver at his words, or read the expression on her face. She wouldn't mind the eerie sound of the wind, the tunnels, or the skeleton, or whatever else, but the bats—

Coming back from the wagon with the lantern, he held it high and peered deeper into the cave. "Don't much like the looks of it back there," he offered. "Don't much like the idea of you going back in there alone, either." Then, much to Sarah's surprise, he said, "Come, we'll go together. Take my hand. I'll lead the way."

The feeling of Michael's strong hand enclosing hers evoked a strange sensation, a tingling in her spine, a sort of flipping motion in her stomach. For a moment she actually felt dizzy. There was little time to try to understand these sensations, however, or to try to decide whether they were pleasant or unpleasant. She felt only his strength, and her need for it.

It was hard-going, once the entrance cavern narrowed into a wide passage way, then into a tunnel not much higher than their heads. Water dripped down from the ceiling here and there, the wetness of the walls making them shine like black marble. It was difficult to avoid the longer stalactites, hanging down from the ceiling like spears.

"I can tell it opens up a ways ahead," said Michael. "Could be another big room of some sort. But after that we'll turn back. No use expecting wood or anything else useful this far in. Best get back to the wagon and what little shelter we have there."

After a few more yards, they emerged into the big room Michael predicted. Swinging the lantern up high and around the walls, Sarah gasped. The uneven light revealed paintings from floor to ceiling, paintings of animals, of hunters on ponies crossing streams and winding single-file through forests after great stags. Other riders rode across waving grass after herds of buffalo. Some riders wore buffalo headdresses, others cascades of feathers. She'd seen them before. They were the same figures on the walls of the Shakota teepees, the same designs of triangles and inter-locking squares on the beaded decorations of their deerskin clothes. Of the very clothes she'd worn as Willhata-nam.

"Oh!" she said, breathless with wonder. "Oh!" Her voice echoed and re-echoed. It was a spiritual place, a ghostly place. "Oh, Michael." Her knees gave out and she sat down abruptly on a large rock near the entrance to the big hall-like room.

"What is it?" he asked, puzzled. "What's the matter?"

"It's them—the Shakota."

"The Shakota? The warriors? You've seen this kind of thing before?"

"Back in their village. The same figures, clothes. Yes, I know them."

Michael looked first at her, then at the painted walls, then back at her. Finally, "What is this place, then?"

"I don't know. But—it looks like a very special place."

"Like a church—a temple?"

"Maybe. Yes, maybe like that. And look, there's a place for a bonfire in the middle of this room. A circle of stones, some half-burnt logs in the center."

"Ah-ha," cried Michael. "*That* we can use. Maybe they won't mind. Plenty of wood outside if they're needing it. Here, take the lantern while I gather up some."

Holding the lantern, Sarah looked more closely at some of the paintings. One in particular drew her attention, a huge buffalo looking so realistic she almost heard his thundering hooves across the prairie. Snatches of memories of Jake, of Sam and Randy. Of their wild galloping after the herd. Of the Shakota raid.

"Hey, there," cried Michael. "Come back here with that lantern." His voice echoed around and around the great room. Hey—hey—hey—

"Help—help—" And "help—help" echoed back fainter.

"Do you need help with that wood, Michael?"

"Course not. Did I ask for it?"

"You did—I heard you."

"No—I didn't!"

They looked at each other. "Who, then—" Michael began, then stopped. As she held up the lantern, Sarah saw a look of fear on his face, a look she'd never seen before. Real and immediate fear. She felt it, too.

"Spirits here—ghosts—we've got to get out of here!" Michael whispered.

"Help—help me! Whoever you are—" Now the voice was louder and came from a tunnel leading out from the opposite side of the cavern.

"Someone or something's down there," Sarah hissed back. "Do you have your gun?"

"Only my hunting knife. Rifle's in the wagon."

"What should we do?"

"It might be a trap," said Michael.

"Who'd want to kill us?"

"Robbers, maybe. I'll try to divert them, while you take the wagon, the team—protect Maw, Sophie—" That he should say this to her!

"Help—over here!" the voice called, sounding fainter this time. *Here—here—here* was the echo.

"Michael! Doesn't that voice sound familiar?"

"Familiar? But hard to tell, so much echo."

"Don't you think we should find out?"

"Well—I don't know if—" Michael hesitated.

"Michael! What if—what if—" She drew in a sharp breath, hardly daring to say it. "What if it's Tom?"

"Tom? Here? In this cave?"

"Yes—what if—" A thousand possibilities raced through her mind. "Michael, listen. When I was in the Shakota village,

Chief Buffalo Thunder said many of the Shakota children were taken away in a raid on the village by the Black Wing. What if Tom was among them? "

"No, that seems unlikely—impossible—"

"Listen to me. Maybe Tom was taken to the Shakota village in the first place, taken by them while out on Boone looking for . . ." she swallowed hard, "looking for me? Then he was forced to go along with the Black Wing and so had to leave Boone behind in the Shakota village."

"How could Tom be here in this cave, then?"

"Maybe he escaped somehow. You know Tom—he was always resourceful—he could have thought of a way. I did."

"Help—help—please—" the voice again. Then a spasm of coughing.

"Sarah and Michael looked at each other. "He sounds like he's sick, needs help," Sarah said.

"Come on. Hold the lantern, and watch your step."

Cautiously they stepped across the uneven floor of the painted cavern and entered a narrow tunnel on the opposite side. They had to crouch down to get through the entrance, but, once through, the tunnel opened out onto a wide rock platform on one side, a sharp drop down into darkness on the other.

"Where are you? Tom, is that you?" called Michael. *You?—you?—you?* echoed against the wet, glistening rock walls. "Here, Sarah—hold the lantern down lower. No, set it down on the ground. Be prepared to run!"

The uncertain light revealed a form lying on the ledge, head and body wrapped in a blanket, lying on a layer of pine branches. The form shifted slightly on the branches, reached out a hand, moaned, and broke into another spasm of coughing.

"Oh, Tom," cried Sarah, "is it you? Really you? Oh, dear Tom, can you forgive me?"

"Tom?" the form asked. "Tom?"

Sarah jumped back, almost falling against Michael "Not Tom? Who—"

"You're not Tom? Tom Kerber?" cried Michael, shocked disappointment in his voice as he bent over to look more closely at the man's face. "Why, it's an old man, bearded. Who are you? How'd you come to be in this place?"

The man moaned, coughed, dropped his hand. "Traveling west. Fell ill on the trail." The man moaned, again. " Some kind settler helped me—shelter here—took my horse—said go for help—"

"How long ago?"

"Don't know—days—days." He broke off, his breathing labored, gasping.

"Sir," said Michael, "we've a wagon back there. Heading out come morning."

"Grateful, young man." The man struggled to talk. "Grateful to you."

"Here, sir, allow me to help you up. Can you stand?" Michael helped the man to his feet, re-wrapping the blanket around him against the damp cold of the cave.

So this wasn't Tom! Sarah was bitterly disappointed. She knew Michael was as well. Yet she was touched by the concern and gentleness which he showed this stranger. And they both knew how difficult it might be to care for him from now on. There was no doctor and little food left.

"Take up the lantern," Michael said to her, "go ahead of us to light the way. I'd hate to fall off this ledge—it's a long way down there."

Sarah picked her way carefully along the ledge, lighting the way ahead of them, with Michael following and supporting the stranger. Slowly, carefully, they picked their way through the low tunnel and across the great painted hall-like room.

"Sarah, keep the lantern steady. I'll come back for the firewood later. Take his other arm. He can lean mostly on me."

"Sarah?" questioned the stranger in a choking kind of voice. "Is that your name? But you're a boy."

"No!" Something about this stranger. A strange feeling. A prickly sensation all the way down her spine.

"What are you, then? If you are Sarah, let me see your face.'"

Surprised, Sarah raised the lantern, its light so close it hurt her eyes.

"Pearl!" gasped the stranger. "My precious Pearl."

It was impossible!

And it was impossible for Sarah to remember exactly what happened next. Somehow Michael on his own half-carried the stranger out to the wagon at the mouth of the cave. Somehow Michael—probably with his mother's help—managed to get this stranger into the wagon, where he was bundled in quilts and spooned hot sassafras tea by Mrs. Kerber. And somehow she, William Lundgren's own Pearl, now sat beside him on the wagon floor, supporting his head while she continued spooning the tea into his mouth and wiped away the dribbles, helping him sit up to ease his breathing.

"Pearl," the man murmured simply, "my own, my dearest Pearl." He fell back, exhausted, against the quilts.

It was only then that Sarah realized this moment was real. That this man was truly her father. That her father was now lying in the Kerbers' wagon. "Pearl," he murmured again, "my precious pearl. I've found you, found you at last."

"Papa," she said, not knowing what to say. Only "Papa, Papa," came out, over and over again.

Finally she knew what to say. What she needed to ask. "Papa, where were you all that time? Why are you here? How did you get here?"

Before he could answer, however, Mrs. Kerber looked in on them. "Now, Ss-sarah Pearl," she cautioned, "he needs to rest. Let him rest a ss-spell. I'm sure you've much to ss-say to each other. Come out now, ss-sit by the fire and eat ss-something. Michael's caught a few quail in a ss-snare, they'll go nicely with the last of my corn pone."

They'd nearly finished when Mrs. Kerber descended down from the wagon to come sit next to Sarah. To Sarah's utter amazement, she took her hand in hers, a dry hand, a coarse hand. "Michael, I'm ss-sure you can make yourss-self useful elsewhere, ss-son. Sophie's all right, asleep in the wagon, next to Mr. Lundgren. I need to talk to Ss-sarah Pearl. And we'd prefer to be alone."

"Talk to me? Alone?" This coming from the Widow Kerber—she could hardly believe her ears.

And so began the answers to Sarah's long unanswered questions. There was, no doubt, still some coolness in Mrs. Kerber's manner, still some hesitation in speaking out. For a full three or four minutes she simply sat, staring at the fire, holding Sarah's hand, twisting her fingers with hers. There was no way Sarah could prompt her, encourage her to speak. It was as if she was again cast under a spell, forcing to wait to hear what she had so long wanted to hear. What had happened to her father?

At last, with a decisive squeeze, Mrs. Kerber cleared her throat. "You ss-see, your father was concerned about you."

"About me?"

"Yes-ss, and about himss-self, of course. He didn't know how you were going to manage without him."

"Without him? Why, where was he going?"

Mrs. Kerber hesitated, let go Sarah's hand, got up, and poked thoughtfully at the fire with her stick. "Going nowhere, except into an illness which might be very serious-ss."

"An illness? He was worried about being sick?"

"Yes, he'd developed an illness-ss during his war years-ss. You knew that. It was ss-slow in coming at first. Then just after your mother died, it took a turn for the worse. Just before Mr. Kerber and I left Ohio—with the children—and joined the Johnson wagon train, I received a letter from your father."

"But how did you—"

"How did we happen to know each other?" She smiled faintly. "Couss-sins, you ss-see, actually very distant couss-sins. We had the ss-same great-grandparents back in Ohio."

"But the letter—what did it say?"

"It wasn't good news-ss at all. He wrote about your mother's death, about Jason. But he was most concerned then about his own illness-ss and how you could manage it and, no doubt, the fact it ss-seemed to be getting wors-sse. He didn't want to worry you. Without telling you he planned to go down to St. Mary's Hospital in Rochester. He'd heard such good things-ss about them." She shook her head. "Oh, he ss-seemed to be ss-so full of hope."

"Why didn't he tell me? I could have helped!" Sarah felt a momentary wave of resentment.

"He didn't want you to fret over him, I guess-ss. In any cas-sse, he told my Arthur and me, with Michael, Tom, and Sophie, to stop in Four Corners and ss-see him. By then he hoped to know whether he ss-should borrow a horse and buggy and travel down to Rochester for some kind of—well some notion about his illness."

"But he disappeared a couple of weeks before you got to Four Corners."

"That's true. By the time we got there, no one knew where he was. We had written Mr. Bergstrom to send a telegram to the hospital. He wasn't there."

"Wasn't there?"

"No." She paused, took out a hankerchief and dabbed at her eyes. "Never expected my husband to pass on before we got to Four Corners. Never did." It was a few moments before she collected her emotions enough to continue.

It was the first time Sarah had ever seen Mrs. Kerber express any real emotion with regard to Mr. Kerber's loss. Or indeed, any other crisis. She'd just taken it stoically, as if it were a matter of course. That was nothing like Papa's reaction when Mama died—And yet, Sarah remembered Mrs. Kerber's emotions when Sophie nearly drowned, whenever she spoke of Tom. There was so much more to the woman than she'd thought. So much more to her father's story than she'd ever imagined.

"Meanwhile, the Johnson wagon train had to move on and left us," Mrs. Kerber continued. "As the days passed, we realized we couldn't leave you all alone there in Four Corners. Mr. Bergstrom dropped an indiscreet word or two about your—er, your financial situation, your dependency upon neighbors whose generosity appeared to be wearing thin. The only thing to do was to take you with us." She threw another piece of wood into the fire, stirred the embers with her stick, and looked directly at Sarah. "Do you underss-stand what we have done, and why?" Without waiting for Sarah's answer, she added, "Now I should look in on William again."

"Wait— Please, Mrs. Kerber!" There were still so many unanswered questions. "What you were whispering about at Bergstrom's store—the money?"

"Well, if you saw any money, it was what was left in your Papa's account at the ss-store. Mr. Bergstrom thought it best for me to take it and keep it for you, just in cas-sse—" she didn't finish, but Sarah knew what she was about to say.

"But, please, where has Papa been? And how did he come to be here—in this cave?"

"As-ss for your Papa's whereabouts-ss, how he came to be here on the trail, well, we've yet to find that out. I expect he'll tell us-ss in good time. Right now, though, I need to ss-see whether he's resting all right." She turned away, her shoulders shaking as she walked toward the wagon. "At least he's found—but not my Tom. Not my poor, darling Tom!"

Sarah was stunned. In her fears over her father's disappearance, her anger against the Kerbers, not understanding the situation at all, she hadn't treated them like she should have. Mrs. Kerber had been concerned about her, unwilling to leave her all alone. And she'd had her own problems. Three children, Mr. Kerber's passing away, losing the Johnson wagon train which could have provided a lot of help and protection.

Hardly aware of what she was doing, Sarah jumped up and put her arms around Mrs. Kerber. "Please forgive me," she said, "oh please, please forgive me."

She never thought she'd ever hear herself say that. But she did.

Chapter 9

DISASTER STRIKES

"TWO more days at most," said Michael early next morning when they were ready to leave the cave. Relief was in his voice and the way he held his shoulders back. "Hup, Hup, boys," he called to Big Horn and Blue. "Last leg—come on, one last effort!"

Sarah sat beside him on the driving bench as the team strained the wagon out of the cave entrance and up the slope leading up to the trail they'd left the day before. "Do you mean that for sure? That's hard to believe!" The image of fat old Mr. Bergstrom waving his white handkerchief as their wagon pulled away from his store came to mind. "Seems like forever since I first got into this wagon, with Tom, in the back." She tried not to let her mind dwell on the subject of Tom. Instead, she added, "You know, Michael, so much has happened since then, hasn't it?"

When Michael didn't reply—he still found communication difficult—Sarah reflected for a few moments on many of those happenings. Each one seemed vividly fixed in her mind. And each one had changed her view of things, little by little. She thought it best not to go into much detail, either to her father or to Michael. Especially to Michael. No telling how he might take it. Would he think her brave or just plain stupid?

Right now, however, at this very moment, sitting beside him, her world seemed very different from those moments back at Bergstrom's store. The people in that world, too.

Perhaps she should change the subject to something more comfortable. "How far have we come, then?"

"Hard to know exactly. I was guessing distances best I could every day. It's not always easy, but—" he broke off. "Hey, hang on—looks like a few rough spots ahead."

Sarah grabbed the wire railing at the end of the bench and braced her feet against the front board. She was used to rough spots. She'd been through so many. It seemed she'd traveled more miles than those hundreds of miles Michael kept track of, and she wanted to share this notion with him. The fact that she wanted to share any thoughts at all with him surprised her. She never thought she'd be able to talk to him like that, or even that he'd listen.

"Can I tell you something?" she began, a little hesitantly.

"What's that?" Although he seemed to be concentrating on managing the ox team over the rough ground, she sensed he was interested and prepared to listen.

"Well, you'll probably think this silly." He didn't comment. "You know, it seems to me, in my mind, I've been to the end of the world and back."

"Why's that?" He glanced at her, then smiled.

"It's because I've been suffering from crazy ideas, crazy things that made me mad. A long, long way, so many things I imagined. Imagining things about people. About you."

"About me? What kind of things?"

She couldn't admit she'd at first found him stuck-up and nasty, that he annoyed her, put her down. Instead, she said, "Well, you see, I didn't know you very well."

"Been right here, all the time."

"That's not what I mean. What I mean is, I now see what a big job you've had, driving the wagon all this way. It can't have been all that easy. And I know you're hurting from losing your father and all that."

At first he made no comment about that. Finally, after another command or two to the oxen, he said, "Men don't admit to hurting."

"Why not? You've got feelings, haven't you?" She laid her hand on his arm. "Look, Michael, we all hurt from things like that. I can't begin to tell you about how I felt—still feels—about Mama." For a moment she couldn't go on and Michael glanced at her, questioningly. "Well, I didn't really want to bring that up. No, we were talking about you, remember?"

"You were saying I seem different?"

"Since yesterday, anyway. After I rode up on Boone and met you on the trail, you never came right out and blamed me for Tom's loss. Yet we both knew very well it was my fault. And then you helped find Papa in the cave." This was becoming more difficult than she'd expected. She needed to change the subject again.

"Well, I guess the most important thing was finding out about Papa."

"Knew that."

"Why didn't you tell me?"

"Weren't sure how to say it. Still some questions, anyways."

"Where he was all that time? How sick he is now?"

"Guess so."

"And now Papa's come all these hundreds of miles just to find me."

"Sure did take a big chance."

"An awful big chance. He'd never have found me except for a miracle. He could have died back there in that cave before the man came back, like he promised."

"Maybe we'll meet him on the trail, whoever he was. That is, if he wasn't heading back in the opposite direction." He looked off in the distance for a minute. "And that is, of course, if nothing's happened to him meantime. Your Paw weren't sure how long it'd been."

"Say, do you think we'll be able to find a doctor for Papa in Discovery?"

"No way of knowing. Depends what settlers are already there in Discovery. At that depends on whether the Johnson train made it." He reflected for a moment. "You know, lots of things can happen . . ."

"I know, Michael. No need to spell them out."

"I'm trying to remember who all was in that wagon train. Seem to recall there was a doctor, but then why couldn't he help my Paw?"

"Is there a chance we could still catch up with them?"

"Doubt it. Too many delays, time lost."

Sarah turned away, embarrassed. She knew delays were largely her fault.

"Hope we make good time now, though. Food's running so low. Unless I get a rabbit or two for tonight, maybe a quail or two, we'll for sure go hungry. All the dried meat, those apples have run out. The hardtack's got weavils—guess you noticed."

He paused to flick the whip at Blue again. "That critter's sure slowing down. Hup, there, hup, hup! All right, you were asking 'bout a doctor. Hope we find one, like I said. But you know,

Maw's pretty good at tending to your pa back there in the wagon. Come the first rest stop, guess you can take over from her."

Then turning to look at her, he said with a half sort-of smile, "Still, though, maybe we could have another miracle."

"Oh? What do you mean, another miracle?"

But when he didn't answer, she thought it best not to press him. Besides, she had her own past miracles to think about, to be thankful for.

That night, sitting next to her father as he lay propped up beside the campfire, Sarah helped him drink the broth Mrs. Kerber had made out of dandelion leaves she'd picked along the trail. "Not too bad, if you swallow it real fast," he remarked, wryly.

"Now, William, I'm doing the best I can," Mrs. Kerber protested. "Managed to pick the weavils-ss out of the last two cups-ss of corn meal, or you wouldn't have much else but dandelion broth."

"I do 'preciate that, Eliza," he said with a smile. "And you can't know how good it tastes, how good to be here, how good to have found you all like this." He paused to take another sip. "Or that you found me." Suddenly he coughed, a rasping sound coming from deep inside his lungs. Sarah helped him sit up more fully to ease his breathing. "Or even, Eliza, to hear your voice again, with your hissing way of talking. I remember that from Ohio, when we were just young sprouts." They both laughed at this, although it brought on another bout of coughing.

"Can't help that, William. Or my bum leg. Hate this old cane, but can't seem to manage without it. It was that accident, you know."

"Can't say as I ever heard 'bout that. But don't you remember when we went down to that old swimming hole in the Ohio River? And we—"

"No, I don't. I do know, though, you shouldn't be talking so much, it's too hard on you. As for my way of talking, well, something's wrong with the way my tongue works, I'm told. Never much I could do about it."

This was news to Sarah. She'd had such different thoughts about Mrs. Kerber—her witch-like appearance, her strange hissing way of speaking, that awful cane. As for her father's health—well, that was now her main concern. He seemed so weak, so frail, not at all like himself.

He wasn't the least like she remembered him. Her last image—what was it? His coming into the kitchen from the south pasture that evening, hanging his old felt hat on the peg, sitting down with her at the table to eat the supper she'd prepared. Bean soup with ham hocks, greens, cornmeal mush, blackberry cobbler. *Delicious, Pearl, just hit the spot. You'll be a great cook someday, make somebody a fine, fine wife!*

Yes, he'd said that. But she hadn't done very well along the trail in Mrs. Kerber's view. Nor Michael's, either. Not well at all. And certainly not among the Buffalo hunters, for that matter. A fine wife—She glanced at Michael, so intent upon keeping the bonfire going, disappearing from time to time to find more wood.

In a way, it reminded her of that night they sat together by the campfire after the James River crossing. Her future—he'd said that'd be her affair. What did he mean by that? Would Michael say something different now? Surely he could never forgive her for losing Tom. She knew it, recognized it every time he stared at her in Tom's green and brown flannel shirt, his overalls.

"That's enough broth, thank you, Pearl," her father remarked, pushing the cup away. "Already feeling better. I'd like to rest now, if you'll help me back into the wagon."

Yes, what were her father's feelings? What were Michael's feelings now? A sudden though struck her. What if her father intended to return to Four Corners? As she helped him stand and supported him while he walked the few steps back to the wagon, she ventured, "When will we go back home? We could maybe head back as soon as you're well. Maybe you could buy this very wagon, since the Kerbers won't need it anymore. I know I can manage it—I know we can make it—I just know—"

William Lundgren looked at her strangely. "Home?" he asked. "No, Pearl, let's not talk about that just yet. I've something to tell you, but it must wait."

He slowly climbed into the wagon, using the wheel spokes by way of a ladder, and pushed aside the canvas. "Now I'll bid you good night. You'll be all right out here? I see Eliza's laid out some quilts near the fire for you, her, and Sophie. Michael, I understand, will be with me in the wagon, in case I need anything during the night. That should allow you a better rest, don't you think? So good night, my dear Pearl!"

But what about Michael? Sarah thought, as she lay down beside Sophie, already fast asleep. He's the one in charge, he's the one driving the wagon. She had another worry, however, and that was her father's strange response with regard to heading back along the trail east to Four Corners. Something about the way he refused to talk about it, the way he looked when he said it.

She'd ask him about that later. Maybe tomorrow—their last leg of the journey. Michael thought they could reach Discovery day after tomorrow by nightfall. They might be hungry when they got there, but they'd finally—and at last—arrive!

Yet there was another part to that worry. Her own feelings about returning to Four Corners. If only she didn't feel so hungry right now, if only her stomach would stop growling. She wanted to talk to Michael, but he was inside the wagon with Papa. She hesitated talking to Mrs. Kerber. It was still an uncomfortable relationship. But just know she had to talk to somebody.

"Mrs. Kerber," she began, "do you think—"

"It's all right to call me Aunt Eliza, Ss-sarah Pearl, now that you know the truth. I'm really not your aunt—well, maybe two or three times-ss back, but that doesn't matter. I'm only ss-sorry it comes-ss so late. But in his letter, the one he ss-sent just before Mr. Kerber and I ss-started on this trip, your father made me promise not to mention his illness-ss."

"Well, then, umm—Aunt—umm, will he recover, do you think?" Calling her aunt was never going to be easy.

"I'm no doctor," she said curtly, "but he's a ss-strong man, with a ss-strong will. This trek west has weakened him, already weak by that long illness-ss he picked up during the war. Got to his lungs-ss. Let's-ss hope with res-sst, the good fresh air coming off those mountainss just the other side of Dis-sscovery—let's hope he'll turn 'round." She rolled over to tuck Sophie in more firmly. "Now we need our rest—ss-so, good night."

Next day, however, offered no opportunity for Sarah to question her father. Or even talk more seriously to Michael. "How much longer, now, do you think," she asked after an hour or so on the trail.

"Hmm—dunno," he mumbled, concentrating on egging on old Blue, who seemed to be stumbling more often.

"Shouldn't we stop, give the team a rest?"

"Can't stop now. Got to keep going."

"But Michael—"

"No, I said. "Got to keep them oxen moving. Once they stop, maybe can't get them to respond. We'd be stuck then. We couldn't—"

She understood what he was trying to tell her, so she left off questioning him, her anxiety rising all the time at what he'd implied.

Later, changing positions with Mrs. Kerber—it was still difficult to call her Aunt, she went back to tend to her father while Mrs. Kerber took Sophie up to the driving bench with Michael. Sitting beside him as he lay on the straw mattress, she kissed his forehead and took his hand. "Papa, are you feeling any better?"

"Yes, dear Pearl, a little."

"We're almost there, Papa."

"I know. I heard you talking to Michael earlier. He's a fine young man."

"Do you think so?" This was a question she needed to pursue.

But to her disappointment, her father only sighed and closed his eyes, saying, "If you don't mind, my dear, let's talk about that later. I'd like to rest a spell."

Mid-morning, Michael was forced to draw the wagon to a stop at a small clearing in the woods along the trail. The storm the previous day had left everything fresh and green, although Sarah noticed a few maples showing brilliant orange in their top branches. "Look at that," she commented to Michael.

His answer was, in a way, a shock. "What else can we expect, now that it's getting into fall? Comes earlier this part of the country, I'm told."

"I guess I've just lost all track of time," she answered lamely. How true. She simply hadn't taken in the fact that so many events happening from Bergstrom's store to this moment in time all added up to many, many moments, many days, several months. Yes, it would soon be fall, and she tried to visualize what she remembered about the brilliant beauty of that season back in Four Corners. But this line of thought steered her into painful depths, and she quickly changed the subject.

She and Michael were sitting on a fallen log near a small spring, where the oxen were snorting, blowing, and drinking their fill. She waited for Michael to say something, anything, but realized she'd have to prompt him. "Michael, what are you thinking about?"

He hesitated, picking up a fallen leaf or two from the grass. "I was thinking about Tom."

This was not going to lead to a satisfactory conversation, either. Before she could divert it to something more comfortable, however, he looked directly at her and continued.

"You can't tell me anymore about Tom or what you saw in that Shakota village?"

"No," she said, "other than what I've already said. Finding Boone in their corral was the only sign the Shakota ever had any contact with him."

"But you said the Black Wing had raided the village and taken away a number of older children?"

"There was nothing to go on that Tom had been among them, no trace . . . except Boone."

"I see. Well, you know what I'm thinking?"

"Yes?" she asked eagerly. It was clear he wanted to talk about Tom. She recognized that his grief over Tom's loss went very deep, so talking about it might help.

"I'm thinking Discovery's not too far from Ft. Buford, up north a ways along the Missouri River. Heard tell the army's built up troop numbers there. Maybe they'd be willing to send a search party out among the Black Wings. Or maybe a scout to nose around for information."

"Would they do that? For only one lost boy?"

"Maybe. Suppose others went missing too? Leastways, I'll think on it. But first, I've got to get us settled at Discover. Find a doctor for your Paw."

Sarah nodded in agreement, hoping it concealed her own feelings of doubt. She was afraid to raise her hopes, either with regard to Tom or to Papa.

By late afternoon they'd crossed the last rolling expanse of prairie. Low hills, laced with brightly colored rocks, rose up in the distance. "Hills—just like before, only bigger and strange looking." She sat with Michael as he drove while the others remained back in the wagon. "Just like before, when we came to the James. Does that mean there's another river just beyond them?"

"No, not yet, anyway. Know the big Missouri lies ahead, but not quite sure where. Trying to remember the map."

"What map?"

"Way back when we started, 'fore we left Ohio. Mr. Johnson, the wagon train captain, laid one out on a table, Paw and I looked at it. He explained the trail and all, what we'd run into. Said it'd be easy-going, flat prairie for the most part."

"You believed him?" By now he should know better.

Michael laughed his wry kind laugh. "Little did he know! I'm sure he's found out for himself by now—that is, if any of them have survived." He broke into a few snorts, flicked his whip at the team, and said nothing more for the next few miles.

Sarah was a little surprised at this show of cynicism and how his mouth twitched from time to time. She was convinced Michael had changed during the course of this trek. But was it for better or worse? It disturbed her to think that day after day of effort and anxiety, of hardship, of responsibility might have taken their toll.

Against her better judgment, she decided to probe a little more deeply into his feelings. Maybe that would help. "Listen, Michael, there's something I'm curious about."

"Oh." Did this response give her license to continue?

"Why'd you decide to make this trek—leave everything, risk everything?" It was a question she'd often asked herself during her journey with the Kerbers. It didn't seem to make sense. The Kerbers had family and a good farm back in Ohio.

He took several minutes to decide whether to answer or not. Finally, still looking straight ahead, he said, "Land—lots of it. Chance to do more, make more, be successful. Leastways, that's what my Paw claimed." Another snorting kind of laugh. "Little did he know he'd never make it."

"What was your father like, then?"

Another long pause. "A good man. In the war, like your Paw. Ohio regiment. Didn't change him much, though, according to Maw. It was the accident that changed him."

"He had an accident?"

"With Maw. Going into town, taking some of our tomatoes, corn, into Saturday market. Just after Sophie was born, left her with me and Tom and my aunt. Horse reared, wagon tipped over." He stopped, hesitating. "Maw's leg got crushed underneath. Took a long time before she could walk again."

"I'm sorry." Sarah wondered what else she could say. This revelation explained some things, why Mrs. Kerber walked with a cane, maybe even why she sometimes acted the way she did. "Does it still pain her?"

"Dunno 'bout that. I expect it does, though Maw—she never complains." He grew thoughtful. "Bigger pain was in Paw's mind. Always there, made him moody. Maybe another word for that pain was guilt. Always felt he'd caused it, somehow."

Guilt. Sarah looked at him in surprise. She knew about guilt. She knew her own sense of guilt came from Jason's drowning—her fault. She'd had to carry that pain in her head all this time. Surely Michael would understand her feelings. They could share them. But how to express it? She wasn't ready to find the words. It was a relief when Michael changed the subject.

"But you were asking 'bout them hills. Far as I recollect, they're supposed to be more like cliffs, strange rocks with deep canyons in between. Mr. Johnson called them the Badlands, warned about staying well on the trail going through."

Sarah shivered at his description. "Don't like the name at all."

"Well, can't do much 'bout that, can we? Just take his advice, I guess, keep well to the trail, however bad it gets." He looked closely at the ox team in front of him, struggling against their yoke through the deep ruts of the trail. "What with Blue so poorly, that'll not be easy."

Once they entered the Badlands and Sarah saw the first pass down over a narrow trail along a steep drop into the canyon below, she realized the truth of Michael's description. The trail was only the width of the wagon, clinging to the rocky cliff-side. Every once in a while as they descended downward, rocks along the outer edge of the trail crumbled away and fell with a hollow echo into the bottom of the canyon below.

"Hang on tight, Sarah," Michael warned. "And be prepared to use the brake lever if it looks like we're slipping sideways."

She was thankful she'd already had some practice braking. Yet lacking Tom's help with the wheel chocks, she realized it was going to be more difficult, much more dangerous. Much more was depending on her and her alone.

It happened near the end of the day. Just when light began to fail. They were making their way down a steep part of the trail toward the bottom of a canyon, where Michael thought they might camp for the night—their last night before reaching the settlement at Discovery and the end of their journey along the trail west.

Just before heading down, he'd suggested that his mother walk behind the wagon, and that Sarah's father ride Boone, holding Sophie. Not that it was easy for Mrs. Kerber to walk any distance, needing her cane as she did. But it would lighten the load. The trail was so rocky and uneven in places that the wagon at times slid dangerously too close to the edge. The oxen needed all their remaining strength to keep it steady.

With both hands on the brake lever, ready to throw it the instant needed, Sarah watched anxiously every inch of the trail. "It's getting almost too dark to see, Michael," she cried out.

"Know it, but we've got to make it down to the bottom, can't stop here. Just keep a sharp lookout. Get's much darker, you may have to walk ahead with the lantern."

"I can see a bad turn ahead, 'round the edge of this cliff!"

"I see it! Whoa, there boys! Steady, steady, not so fast! Sarah, get ready to brake as we take the turn! Trail looking narrower there. It'll be awful tricky."

Just as the team veered left to take the turn, there was a loud rumbling sound. "Michael—Michael!" yelled Sarah. "Brakes not working—wagon's back wheel is sliding right off the trail!"

"Rockslide! Can't keep it steady!" He flicked his whip at the team, "Hup! Hup! If I can pull ahead, try to get the rear wheels back onto the trail—"

"We're falling," she screamed, "falling down—"

"Jump, Sarah! Jump clear!" He dropped the reins and threw his arms around her, and together they rolled off the driving bench and hit the ground just as the wagon and the team with it disappeared over the edge of the trail down into the canyon below.

There was a bellowing from the oxen and a horrible scraping, crashing sound—splintering of wood, the iron kettle clanging over and over again as it broke loose and bounced all the way down to the bottom of the canyon against the rocks. A shower of loose rocks followed.

"Under here, Sarah!" Michael shouted, half-carrying, half-dragging her. "Get under this ledge." Above their heads rocks continued to roar down, some as big as boulders. Together he and Sarah crouched under a projecting rock, kept in place by several tree roots.

"Oh, oh—Michael—Papa—" was all Sarah could say out of shock and fear. A horrible confusion of earth and rocks moving all around them, the crashing sounds of the wagon and all its contents, the panicked bellowing of the oxen.

The thunder of falling rocks slowed. After what seemed like an eternity they stopped, all except the slight grumbling of last bits of rock and gravel spilling down the cliff into the canyon below. When that stopped, a deadly silence.

"Pearl—Pearl—" came a faint voice. The whinny of a horse.

"It's your father, Sarah," said Michael. He crawled out from under the ledge and stood on what was left of the trail. Sarah was right behind him. "Maw! Mr. Lundgren! Are you all right?"

Scarcely audible above Sophie's screaming, Michael's mother answered, "Thank goodness we weren't in the wagon—

we'd be gone for sure. And poor old Boone, too, if he'd been tied behind it." She looked cautiously over the edge of the cliff down into the darkness below. "But—oh—the wagon! The wagon's los-sst! What'll we do?" She hugged Sophie closer and began to cry herself. It was not the first time Sarah had seen her break down, but this was somehow different. It involved neither Sophie nor Tom, but simply disastrous circumstances over which she had no control.

"Now, Eliza," said William Lundgren above Sophie's screams, as Boone, obviously terrified, cautiously placed one hoof at a time along the narrow ledge which was all that was left of the trail, "we're all still alive!" They stopped as they came up to Michael and Pearl. "Yes, alive—that's all that matters!"

"Wait, Maw," said Michael, "I'll help you over this pile of loose rocks. Still got your cane? Good. Mr. Lundgren and Sophie can ride Boone down, but do you think you can walk the rest of the way?"

"I can try, ss-son," she answered, appearing pale and shaken. But with a sudden toss of her head, she added, "We've managed so far, haven't we? But I wish it weren't getting dark ss-so soon. It won't make it any easier."

"Just keep as close to the cliff as you can, right behind Sarah and me. And, Mr. Lundgren, I think you can trust old Boone—he's got good horse-sense when it comes to sensing the ground under his hooves, even when there's not much light."

After nearly half an hour in growing darkness, the group managed to pick their way safely down the trail to the canyon bottom. There had been a few close-calls from rocks breaking loose under foot, or occasional showers of debris from above. Each time a rock fell, Sarah felt terror rise. She felt quite weak in the knees by the time her worn boots felt the level, grassy verge along the canyon floor. With relief she watched Michael helping her father and Sophie down off Boone.

"You lie here on the grass, sir," he said, "and rest."

"What about you?" William Lundgren asked shakily, then immediately broke into a fit of coughing.

"While there's still some light, I've got to go find what I can from the wreck of the wagon."

"I'll go with you ," Sarah insisted. That is, if Aunt umm . . . Mrs. Kerber . . . er Aunt Eliza . . . can manage with Papa and Sophie."

"Yes, Ss-sarah Pearl," she said, "go on. Michael probably needs-ss your help. No ques-sstion but what night's-ss coming on and we're running out of time. Firs-sst thing we'll need is-ss ss-something to build a fire with."

Picking their way carefully along several hundred feet of canyon floor, Michael and Sarah came to where most of the wagon had landed. First they discovered fragments of wood, smashed to bits on the rocks. Then a coil of rope. One shattered wheel hung from a tree growing out of the cliffside, another lay surprisingly intact on the rocks below. Clothing lay scattered all around, along with pots, pans, broken dishes, and various tools.

A loud bellowing led them to where Big Horn lay on his side, threshing in pain among the bushes and fallen rocks, the remains of the wooden yoke still around his neck. "Where's Blue?" Sarah asked, shuddering at his pathetic state.

"Just over there," said Michael, pointing toward a clump of low pine trees. "Poor beast didn't make it." He took a closer took at Big Horn and passed his hand along the ox's exposed shoulder. "Looks like he didn't either. Both front legs are broken."

"Oh, no!" She knew what that meant. "You'll have to—"

"Afraid so—soon's I find the rifle."

For another ten minutes or so they walked cautiously through the wreckage. "Got the tinder box, the frying pan, food tin with what's left of last night's corn pone," shouted Sarah. "And here's a couple of quilts!" She loaded the items into one of the quilts and slung it over her shoulder like a bag.

"And here's the rifle," said Michael. "Now you take what you've found back to the others, while I do—what I have to do."

Sarah knew what was coming. She hurried away quickly, despite so much to carry, and tried not to hear the two rifle shots. They echoed again and again throughout the narrow canyon until she thought she was going to scream.

It was only then, with the sound of those terrible, echoing rifle shots, that she realized the full impact of the present situation. Both oxen gone. The wagon destroyed. It was now almost totally dark, and they'd recovered very little to make camp with. They were at the bottom of a deep canyon. There was no way to go on. There was no way to go back. They were going—nowhere.

Chapter 10

FRAGMENTS OF HOPE

THE night was cold, and dampness seeped up from the ground and down from the canyon walls. A chilling wind howled through the narrow canyon like a siren, joined by the song of wolves high up on the ridge. Had there been moonlight, Sarah knew she'd see their dark forms against the sky. She shivered, glad Michael kept a campfire going. Glad they had been able to locate the flint box, still intact. Even so, he'd soon be leaving to keep watch by her father during the long night ahead. Michael had discovered an overhanging rock a short distance away providing some shelter for them both and layered the ground with spongy cedar branches and sage.

Once Michael was gone, Sarah would have to keep the fire going. At the moment, its surging flames cast a more cheerful look around them, huddled as they were in whatever quilts, whatever clothing, they'd managed to recover after the scattered wreckage of the wagon all over the canyon floor.

"Fire's some comfort," Michael remarked, throwing down his last armload of pine branches. "Leastways we've been able to boil water in that old iron frying plan and make some coffee. Although can't say it was any substitute for supper, but come morning, it'll go down even better." He laid on some more wood and the flames shot up as if struggling to reach the stars overhead. "Will you look over there—Maw and little Sophie already asleep, rolled up in those quilts. Plumb tuckered out, I 'spect. Proud of my little sis, though. Apart from being scared to death and hollering like the dickens when that cliff came down on us, she hasn't complained. You neither, Sarah." He glanced at her, a guarded compliment in his tone.

"I have to say," Sarah confessed, "it happened all too quickly to be afraid. I guess I just didn't think about complaining with so much to do afterwards." Her main concern had been for her father, frail as he was. No, the real truth was, concerned about all of them. She just didn't know how to say it, or admitting it, especially to Michael.

"I need to go over and check on your paw. If he seems all right and doesn't need anything, or he's already asleep, maybe I'll just lie down beside him and get some rest myself. Feeling a bit tired, however much I keep fighting it." Clearly he hated to admit it. "Are you sure you'll be all right out here?"

"I think so," although she wasn't too sure about that.

" You can keep the fire going?"

"I'll try. You've gathered up quite a bit of stuff. It should last most of the night, anyway." She wasn't too sure about that, either.

"You'll call me if there's any trouble?"

"Yes."

"Any kind?"

"Yes." He seemed reluctant to leave. What was the matter? Did she dare ask? Communication had slowly improved between them during the course of the last two days, but Sarah's instincts told her to handle it carefully and delicately. Michael's communications were still according to his own initiatives and rarely at her prompting.

At that moment, Michael took the initiative. Sitting down heavily beside her, he pulled a corner of the quilt around them both. They sat there together for several minutes in silence, staring at the dancing flames. Sarah waited, aware of the sensation of their closeness, of the quilt enveloping the warmth of their bodies together, the darkness shutting out the world around them. It was the closest she had ever been to him, and it was not difficult to sense that he was deeply troubled and wanted to communicate this to her but was hesitant to do so.

Suddenly Michael buried his face in his hands. She felt his body convulse, as if warding off unwanted emotions. After a few more seconds, with a resolved heave of his shoulders, he straightened up and stared fixedly the fire.

"Michael?" She laid her hand on his knee, knowing it would be improper to do more. "Michael? What's wrong?"

He took her hand in his. Holding it tightly, his gaze still fixed on the fire, he said slowly and deliberately, "I hardly need tell you we're in a difficult situation."

"Yes, I know that."

"You know I had to put Big Horn out of his misery."

"Yes. It could not have been easy."

"After that, there are only two shots left in the rifle."

"Only two? But what about your box of—"

"Lost somewhere down here, probably buried under rocks. May never find it. Just two shots." Now he looked directly at her, and, in the flickering light from the fire, she saw an expression on his face she'd never seen before. Incredulity? Horror? "Do you understand what that means?"

"No, I guess not."

"Two shots?"

What was he driving at? She was at a loss.

"Those two shots must be saved for . . . for . . . for whatever . . ." and he broke off.

Now she understood. Only two shots and they had to be saved for hunting game for food. For defense against wolves or bears, or even mountain lions—they'd already seen two or three up on the cliffs. Trapped down in this canyon they were helpless, with no means of escape. And there were always the Shakota, somewhere, maybe hunting for her. Two shots left, only two.

The pressure of his hand on hers increased. "If only we could figure out some way to get out of here. If only—"

"There must be some way." The fire sparked and popped, as if agreeing with her.

Michael shook his head. "It seems hopeless to me. Although you know me well enough by now to realize I won't give up easily." He paused, looked at her intently, and again squeezed her hand "I know you won't either, Sarah."

It felt good to hear him say this, it was good to feel the pressure of his hand. Sarah looked around her in the darkness, the only light from a few flickering reflections from the fire against the dark, stone walls of the canyon. The only sounds the crackling fire and bone-chilling howls from the wolves up on the ridge above them. Above the prowling wolves, far, far above, the icy glint of stars in the black sky void.

"Best get some sleep, like the others," Michael finally said in a moment of resolve. He released her hand and stood up, tucking the quilt back around her shoulders. As he banked the fire, he said, "Listen Sarah, best try to sleep. You'll need all your strength for tomorrow—for whatever tomorrow brings." He turned to leave, but added, "I'll check your father. But don't worry, I'll come back every once in a while to check on the fire. Besides the warmth, it'll also keep any animals at a distance."

It occurred to Sarah that the campfire might also be a danger. "What about—what about the Shakota? Won't they see it and know we're down here?"

Michael's jaw firmed. "That's something we can't think about. Shouldn't even consider. Not just now." Then he disappeared into the darkness to join her father. She was alone.

Still, the feeling of his hand on hers, somehow reassuring and comforting, seemed to remain with her as she lay back and rolled herself in the quilt, already damp from the night air. Sleep seemed unreachable. Wide awake after at least another hour, her mind raced through idea after idea, situation after situation, possibility after possibility.

She stared at the fire, now burning down to low bluish flames and glowing red embers. The resin in the pine branches hissed and sputtered, sending out sparks some distance. She hoped the fire was not about to give up, as Michael's unspoken words seemed to suggest they would all, all of them, be forced in the end to give up. No, she needed to keep the fire going, but she was too tired and too cold to leave the warmth of the quilt to get up and revive it. Why hadn't Michael come back as he'd promised? He must have dropped off into an exhausted sleep beside her father, and she should not begrudge him that.

Suddenly, in one quick movement, she sat up and threw aside the quilt. An idea flashed through her mind, taking shape in her imagination, shaping an image so clear it seemed real and could be touched with her finger tips. There it was. The solution! Her whole body tingled with excitement, with the excitement of hope.

What had they saved from the wreck of the wagon? What all had they used for the fire? No way to tell, exactly. But she had to stop it burning until she could be sure.

Springing to her feet, she began kicking dirt over the flames. After a few moments only a few dying embers glowed beneath the dirt. Now the darkness all around her was nearly complete. The rest of the night she drifted in and out of an anxious sleep, waiting until she knew the answer to the many questions which the image she'd imagined were beginning to generate.

Next morning, before anyone was stirring, and as a grayish dawn trickled down by degrees into the canyon, she closely examined the place where the fire had burned out. One by one she turned over the charred fragments, examining them closely, then heaved a sigh of relief. There was no evidence of wood from the wagon, only tree limbs. Now was the time to explain things to Michael. In the growing light of dawn she made her way through the scrub bushes to where Michael and her father had spent the night. The overhanging ledge above them formed a protected enclosure against the wind, and the scent of the sage bushes which Michael had gathered gave off an aura of warmth and comfort. It was no wonder they were both still asleep.

"Michael! Michael!" she whispered, so as not to wake her father. "Listen! I've got an idea. A plan!"

With some difficulty Michael shook himself awake. "What—what are you doing? What plan?" he asked, dazedly.

"I've got a plan," she repeated. "Come quietly. Let's not wake the others. Will you get more branches and re-start the fire?"

"Why? You let it go out?"

She couldn't explain, not just yet. "Meanwhile, I'll take the frying pan and get water from that stream. We'll get some breakfast ready—that is, if you count just coffee as breakfast!"

Glancing ruefully at Boone, grazing nearby, he smiled faintly. "Leastways old Boone over there—he's got grass. Makes no difference to him."

"How fortunate he survived the disaster." Then she added, recalling how the horse had been her means of escape from the Shakota village, her means of reuniting with the Kerber family—and Michael, "By now he seems like an old friend."

Michael nodded. "Maybe more'n that."

What did he mean by that? She hoped it wasn't an allusion to Tom's loss, and her part in it. She needed no reminder, no accusation.

As she knelt down to fill the frying pan with water, she noticed that the stream in the growing daylight was bigger than she'd thought. That was good. Water gushed down from several waterfalls up in the rocks to form a channel growing wider as it headed out the far end of the canyon. She ran after Michael, now some ways off gathering up branches, fragments of the wagon to burn. Now she could tell him about her plan. Now was the time.

"What's left of the wagon?" she asked, out of breath

"Well, tailgate, couple of boards from the side, axles with a couple of metal pins, that broken wheel. Not sure where the other three are. Why?" he asked in surprise. "No earthly good, 'cept to keep us warm and boil water for coffee."

"No, Michael. I've an idea, a plan, like I said. You'll think it silly, but—" And so she told him what she had seen in her vision.

"Impossible—it'll never work." He shook his head in disbelief. "Your imagination, Sarah, is one thing. What we can actually do with it is another."

"Do we have other choices?"

He hesitated. "Guess not."

For the rest of the morning, she and Michael searched among the rocks and brush for anything they could find. Sophie insisted on helping, although she had a tendency to wander out of sight, which made Sarah nervous.

"Look, Sawah! Hat!" Sophie cried at one point. She emerged from behind a bush along the canyon wall proudly waving her father's old, straw hat. "Hat no good," she insisted, "big hole." Sarah was tempted to relate the hat incident in the Shakota village to Michael, but thought better of it, and so smothered its memory in a faint smile.

By noon they'd recovered a pile of wood fragments—some large, most of them small—and other odds and ends. These included the old chest, which, by some miracle, had rolled down and landed in a clump of sagebrush, all in one piece, except for broken lid hinges. Sarah searched through it for anything useful, finally deciding, reluctantly, to leave everything behind—including her carpetbag with her best dress, the pink silk. But first she looked through it to find the leather bag of money belonging to Aunt Eliza—it might be useful. She knew her mother's locket was gone, but, in a way, felt little sorrow for its loss. Its loss had in fact given her something more valuable.

They set to work on Sarah's plan. "Do you think that will work?" Her father sounded skeptical as he, now awake and sitting beside the rejuvenated campfire, began to sip the mug of coffee Mrs. Kerber handed him.

"We have to try, Papa. And we have to be able to get back home—at least try to get back home—to Four Corners."

He looked at her intently for a moment. Finally he cleared his throat and said, "No Pearl. No use in that." He set the mug down on the grass beside him, rubbing his finger thoughtfully around its edge.

"What do you mean?" His tone alarmed her.

"I've put off telling you. I didn't want to disappoint you." He avoided looking at her, picked up the mug of coffee, took a few more sips.

"Tell me what? How would you disappoint me?" After her joyous reunion with him, this was unexpected, a set back.

"You see, my dear, when I first left you and our homestead back in Four Corners, I hesitated to tell you why. And I expected to return in a few days. And I expected you wouldn't be worried, just think I'd gone up to Green Prairie in connection with some business or other."

"Where did you go that you couldn't tell me? I did worry."

He shook his head. "I know. I regret that, and I'm sorry. Actually, I wanted to go down to St. Mary's Hospital in Rochester. One of the best places in the whole area. They had all sorts of specialists. I was determined to get all the help I could. You see, the last thing I wanted was to become an invalid, a serious burden to you."

"But Papa—"

"No, now listen. One of their army doctors informed me that I couldn't be cured. That the damage to my heart I'd received during the war—that Confederate bullet—could never be helped, would only get worse. Then there was this disease to my lungs called comsumption—I was told any heavy work would probably kill me."

"Oh, Papa! I could have helped!"

"I couldn't let you do that. Not more, at least, than is expected of a woman."

His words struck Sarah as somewhat ironic, given her recent experiences. They'd hardly been expected of a woman! Maybe later, much later, the horrific dangers she'd experienced would fade from memory and she'd be able to talk about them, even to laugh about them. This wasn't the time.

"So, you see, Sarah—and how well that name suits you. I'd never have thought it—so you see, I knew I'd never be able to work the farm adequately again. This was terrible news. I felt especially bad about you and what your future was going to be like. In fact, coming back to Four Corners, feeling so bad about everything, I wasn't thinking clearly and turned up the wrong road."

"You got lost?"

"Worse than that. Our old horse—you remember Storm? Well, it wasn't long before he stumbled and pitched me into a ditch. The accident left him with a broken leg, me with a couple of broken ribs. When I came to, I was being looked after by a farmer and his wife, someplace called South Prairie. I was delirious for a spell, off and on, they said. They said I kept calling your name, over and over. And because of my other conditions, they thought several times I was at the point of dying. At first I wasn't able to tell them who I was. Then, once the delirium passed, they couldn't find anybody to get word up to Four Corners, about a hundred miles away." He turned away slightly and added in a guarded tone, "Poor old Storm, had to be put down."

That was of less concern. "But you made it back."

"A couple of weeks later one of their neighbors had business near there. He kindly took me in his buggy. I was grateful to him, and glad to see the old house again."

"I'd already left. Oh, Papa, if only I'd waited!"

"How shocked I was to see the place deserted and run-down. After I'd asked around, Mr. Bergstrom at the store told me the Kerbers had insisted on taking you with them."

"I wanted to stay, Papa. I tried my best."

Her father was visibly moved. Placing a hand on her shoulder and giving it an affectionate squeeze, he said, "I know you did, my precious Pearl. Perhaps you did the right thing. Perhaps it was the right choice, being with kin, being looked after."

At this Sarah smiled and flung her arms around his neck. "Yes, Papa, I was looked after." He would never know what she really meant by these words.

"In any case," William Lundgren continued, "once I knew Eliza must have felt she couldn't leave you there alone, without any means of support, without knowing what had happened to me all those weeks, and that she'd persuaded you to go with them, I had no choice."

Persuaded is hardly the word, thought Sarah. She left him for a moment to replenish his mug, then settled back down by his side. "But, go on, Papa. You're going to tell me that you had no choice but to come after them, and bring me home? Oh, if only I'd waited!" she repeated.

"That's right. But, you—nobody—could have known. Anyway, I negotiated with some folks. Didn't have any trouble selling the homestead the next couple of weeks, using some of the money to buy a horse, put the rest in the bank for whatever future there might be. Then there was nothing to do but head out after you. I knew you'd be with the Johnson train by them, so it wouldn't be too difficult to trace you. It was only a question of how my health would hold out. I hoped beyond hope—"

"Papa, Papa!" she threw her arms around him once again and held him close. "You did find me. You're here. That's all that matters!" Nevertheless, she felt torn. Could she admit to him that there was something that mattered, how grieved she was to learn their old homestead was sold? Only its memories were left. There would be nothing to go back to. Even her mother's locket was was now only a memory, intangible, soon fading into the distant past.

"I'm sorry, my precious Pearl. I can't tell you how sorry I am for all your anxiety, how much I regret your suffering. But yes, as you said, we are here. And the truth is, there'd be little to go back to. Perhaps—who knows—perhaps if we're able to make it out of this infernal canyon—" He stroked his beard thoughtfully. "Perhaps even find my brother Jack. I only know they came out here to claim a homestead, somewhere west, either Dakota Territory or Montana. But it'd be like finding a needle in a haystack. And we've got about the same chances of survival here."

"But, Papa," she insisted. "That's exactly what I'm trying to do, trying to tell you. Don't you see? We're going to make a raft out of what's left of the wagon. And then we're all going to get on it and float it downstream out of here."

He looked at her in astonishment. "A raft? Out of that?" He pointed to the pile of fragments. "I don't see how—" he stroked his beard thoughtfully again, a gesture Sarah had so often seen. "I don't see how you can put all that together, together in such a way as it will float. Let alone have room for all of us." Shaking his head doubtfully, he added, "No, my Pearl, not in a thousand years. And however practical and able you've become through your many days on this journey."

"But isn't it worth a try, sir?" asked Michael, sitting down beside Sarah.

"You'd best try for a miracle," he answered.

"Papa—" Sarah got to her feet and pulled Michael to his. "I know something about miracles. So now, Michael, let's get to work. And, Papa, if you want to help, you can sort out any rope you can find."

He smiled. "I think that may be the simplest part of this scheme. I'll get little Sophie here to help. The rest is up to you— and your vision."

Together Sarah and Michael laid out the wagon's axle beams with the longest surviving boards on each side. Taking bits of rope from the pile her father and Sophie had assembled, they tied the ends together to form a rectangular frame, roughly the shape of the wagon.

"Now how about these long branches on top?" Sarah asked.

"That might work," Michael answered. "Providing there's enough rope. Don't look like it's enough by a long shot."

"How about tearing off strips from the bedding?"

"Might work. Say, Maw, we need you here. Take this quilt—hate to see you ruin it, all that work piecing, but maybe it'll be worth the sacrifice. Here, take my hunting knife, get the strips as long and as strong as you can."

"But ss-son," Mrs. Kerber protested, "don't you ss-see that's all piece-work—I can't get long ss-strips out of that."

"Now, Eliza, if I may make a suggestion?" Sarah's father made an embarrassed cough. "You have somewhere upon your person, I believe, some—er some unmentionables? Good strong linen? Well?"

The sounds of ripping cloth, snapping branches, intermittent directions and re-directions prevented further conversation. By noon a hot sun flooded into the canyon to reveal a strange creation.

"Will you look at that!" Michael exclaimed. "A jig-saw-puzzle of a raft! No, a raft like a piecework quilt, that's what it is! That old tailgate's about the biggest piece we could salvage—rest all fitted around, including some wheel spokes. And that old chest, without the lid—we can fasten that down in the middle. That'd be a good place to put Sophie so she don't fall off."

He stopped to wedge more soft twigs into gaps between the logs. "Have to give you credit, Sarah. Not sure I would've thought of this."

"You might have, Michael, in time, maybe." Sarah replied.

"We don't have much time, ss-son," Mrs. Kerber pointed out. "Now the big question is, will it float?"

"We'll soon see. Come on, Sarah, help me push this ship out into the stream."

"Careful, now," her father cautioned, "I'll keep hold of these—what you might call mooring ropes. Don't let the raft get away. And, say, by the way, mind if I ask a practical question?" Sarah wondered whether he was going to make one of his wry comments.

"Well, Sarah, since you seem to have been in charge of this marvelous plan. Where does this stream lead?"

"Lead?"

"Yes. Lead, go. Once we're on it, and assuming this—er—this ship will float, where will it go? Where will it take us?"

"I—Michael and I—that is, we don't know."

"You don't know? Then do you think we'll be better off? Floating nowhere, maybe just around and around this wretched canyon until we die of—of—" He clearly did not want to specify.

Sarah glanced up at the grim walls of the canyon, remembering the song of the wolves last night—and earlier nights during her wild ride on Boone through the woods escaping from the Shakota village. She imagined possible threats from a hundred other sources. "I don't know, Papa. But Michael and I agree it's worth a try. And you'd be the first to agree, wouldn't you, that miracles do happen?"

He had nothing to say to that. In fact, nothing more was said by anybody until they'd loaded everything they could on the raft. Sophie was put into the chest, along with several quilts for padding, and some of the cooking utensils. Mrs. Kerber insisted one never knew when such things might be useful.

The horse, Boone, stood patiently on the bank, waiting for—clearly he had no idea for what. "Boone—old Boone!" cried Sophie. "Boone come, too!"

And so Boone was loaded onto the rear part of the raft, his reins tied to one of the wheel spokes. From his weight, the raft sank down several inches into the water.

"That horse'll have to be left behind," said Mrs. Kerber.

"No, Maw," Michael insisted. "We're still afloat. Besides, we can't leave him. He's all we have left of—"

Sarah knew he was alluding to Tom. She dared not say anything, but instead assisted Michael in shoving the raft off from the bank by kicking against a large boulder.

Michael gave a final shove with one of the few intact boards and the raft slowly drifted out into the center. Idling and turning lazily from side to side, the current finally caught it and spun it into the middle of the stream, nearly throwing Michael off balance. He steadied himself against Boone just in time.

There was hardly space between the raft and either bank. Often branches snagged the structure, threatening to hold it back, or large underwater rocks scraped against the logs, threatening to tear them apart. Each time Michael, with the one long board saved as a combination oar and rudder, managed to free them. Within about half an hour, the raft had picked up speed. In another half hour it was rapidly approaching the end of the canyon. Immediately in front of them was a vast wall of rock, the height of the canyon.

"What now?" cried Michael. "There's no way out—I don't see any way out!"

"No—look!" Sarah shaded her eyes and pointed ahead. "See those vines hanging down from the cliff? They're covering up some sort of cave—no, not a cave—a tunnel of some sort, right at the level of this stream. Can you see any light at the far end?"

"That tunnel's too narrow to get through." Her father threw up his hands in despair. "No way out, like Michael said. So much for your plan—as the Scottish poet, Robert Burns once said, the plans of mice and men—"

"Well, sir," Michael interjected, "we're not exactly mice or—" he looked at Sarah, "or men, but just maybe . . ."

As they reached the tunnel entrance, Sarah cried out, "Look—I think we can get through! Just barely! It'll be a tight squeeze for Boone, though."

"Should have left him back there," muttered Sarah's father. "Not worth it."

Sarah could not help but think otherwise. After all she and Boone had gone through, after all he meant to the family. No, it was worth it!

By now they were entering the tunnel. "Get ready, Sarah." Michael handed her his long board. "You'll have to push us away on your side from the rocks with this. I'll use my hands and feet on the other side. Good thing we were able to salvage the axle beams—they'll strengthen the log framework if we crash into anything big."

The tunnel narrowed slightly within a few more feet, and within a few feet more its roof clearance was less. "Maw," shouted Michael, "take hold of Boone's reins, pull his head down. Maybe we can just barely scrape through. And watch out the chest don't slide off the raft with Sophie in it!"

There was a period of semi-darkness, a stifling closeness of air. The water roared and echoed. Every time she pushed at rocks, the sound echoed. Sarah experienced moments of fear and regret, fear of dying in this tomb-like watery grave, regret at causing the deaths of the rest of the Kerber family and her own dear father—who, ironically, had come to rescue her.

Slowly the semi-darkness grew lighter, then lighter still. There was the smell of pure, fresh air, mixed with the scent of grass. More long minutes of pushing, twisting, and bumping—and they were through! The stream widened, running through shallow valleys, areas of grassy pastures, reedy swamps. After about an hour, they hit some low rapids which slid them into a much wider and slower-moving body of water, almost like a lake.

"Michael," Sarah asked during this period of calm, "do you have any idea where we're heading?"

"Don't quite know," he answered. "But I'll tell you this much. When we first started out, I could tell by the sun and shadows that we were going west, then we turned southwest. Then we turned again, this time northwest. Now I think we're going west again."

Sarah's father nodded. "That seems right to me."

"Oh, if only we had Mr. Johnson's-ss map," wailed Mrs. Kerber. "Then we'd know for ss-sure."

"We sort of do know, Maw. I'm trying hard to remember it. Now, if I recollect rightly, we're heading west toward the Missouri River."

"And small rivers empty into big rivers!" William Lundgren slapped his thigh. "By George, that's possible! Only problem is, we don't know just where this one's going to come out."

It wasn't long before he had his answer. The raft swirled out of the river into a wide delta, which in turn opened out into a much wider channel, overhung with cliffs on the east side and offering a view of open country on the other. Far, far off in the distance was a range of snow-capped mountains, half-hidden behind low-hanging clouds.

"The Missouri, you think?" Michael asked. "Sure looks like it might be. Fairly swift current. Seems to be taking us north."

"It's the Missouri. I just know it." *At least*, Sarah thought to herself, *I just hope it is.* She realized that, thus far, she'd pushed everyone's confidence and cooperation well beyond what she might have expected, including Michael's. She also realized that, had he not been willing to trust her, to help her, they would never have gotten out of that canyon. They would still be there, their bones eventually bleaching in the sun, the fragments of the wagon a memorial to their courage. Their courage? She hadn't really thought about that. Perhaps, yes, just possibly, courage had been a part of this trail to nowhere. Yes, a big part of it, all along.

Nevertheless, Mrs. Kerber still looked skeptical. "Ss-so what does-ss that mean? What good will that do us-ss? We were told Discovery was ss-somewhere near the Missouri River. Now what if we're floating along in the wrong direction? What if it's-s back ss-south—upss-stream—and behind us-ss? What if—" She threw up her hands in despair.

Clearly Sarah's plan had pushed her too far, had pushed the others too far. Yet Michael had not actually come out and admitted that. She was sure it wouldn't be long before he did, before their growing relationship would dissolve into the dust of broken hopes, or, more appropriately under the circumstances, drowned in surging waters . . . Will-hata-nam . . . Will-hata-nam . . . Why had this name occurred to her?

"Now, Mrs. Kerber," she found herself blurting out, "let's hope for the best." She didn't want to say anymore. She had to be careful in her relationship with this woman, who, she knew, still blamed her for Tom's disappearance. No amount of effort on her part, of helping them survive the canyon and, hopefully—on their way to their goal—could make up for that.

The river flowed on, sometimes in broad curves, sometimes over shallow rapids which the raft managed to get through with a lot of guidance from Michael's long board.

It grew late. Early September dusk began to shroud the river in shadows from stands of trees along the bank. To their left they watched the sun rapidly sink closer to the horizon. The air was definitely turning colder, and patches of mist lay on the water.

"What's that?" Sarah was sure she saw dark forms high up on the cliffs above the river. The forms appeared to be following them. Were they animals? Shakota? Black Wings? Waiting for a chance to attack?

"Look—water come!" Sophie suddenly screamed from where she was standing inside the big chest. She pointed toward her feet and then toward the rear of the raft.

Michael came around to look. "Raft's sitting lower in the water," he observed. "Guess it's getting' waterlogged, or the weight's pushing it under. May have to take Boone off and let him swim along behind."

"How about pulling over to the bank and camping for the night?" Sarah's father was looking very tired.

No one spoke. No one agreed. It seemed to Sarah that everyone was discouraged and about to give up. She knew, they all knew, that they could not survive another night without food, and exposed to any number of dangers. Those figures up along the cliffs. Cold, hunger, despair— What hope did they have?

Chapter 11

CHOICES

IN that moment of despair, Michael stepped across the waterlogged raft and put his arm around Sarah. "It was a great plan, Sarah. It was our only choice. We had no other. And it wasn't a bad one. It isn't your fault that we're—"

"Bacon! Sophie smell breakfast!"

"The child's delirious-ss," sniffed Mrs. Kerber. "No wonder—you and your ideas-ss!"

"By George," shouted Sarah's father, "Sophie's right! I smell bacon, too!"

The raft was dangerously low in the water, with water rushing over their feet and beginning to fill up the chest where Sophie stood. The current was just about to sweep them toward a wide bend in the river.

"Look! Oh, look there!" cried Sarah, pointing ahead as they rounded the bend.

Coming into view was a landing place, with long boards projecting out into the river and several small boats tied up or beached. A man was standing at the end with a fishing pole in his hand. Suddenly spotting the raft, he dropped his pole into the river and shouted something.

"Look there! Tents, log cabins—wagons!" Michael grew more excited.

"It's the settlement—the settlement!" cried Sarah.

"Here, Sarah, take this board," Michael cried. "Use it as a rudder. And you, Maw! Kneel down here on the side of the raft and paddle with your hands like oars. I'll take the other side. No, no, Sarah, wiggle that board back and forth in the water, more to on the right. It'll push us toward that wharf!"

The raft slowing eased itself out of the main current and edged closer to shore. The next moment the settlement came alive, a blur of movement, a chaos of sounds. People began running, shouting, and waving. More joined the fisherman on the landing place, someone shoved a small boat into the water and got behind the oars. Dogs were barking, a woman banged loudly on an iron pot lid, several men rode along the bank calling out instructions—"More to the right"—"No, no, more this way, this way"—"Easy does it!"

"What place? What place is this?" Michael cupped his hands to his mouth, but the reply was drowned out by the gurgling current surging over the base of the sinking raft, Sophie's screams, and the frantic noise from the settlement.

As they slowly neared the wharf, Mrs. Kerber got to her feet. Hanging on to the side of the chest with one hand to steady herself, she pointed with the other to someone on the wharf. "Oh, I see him! There he is!"

"Who?" Sarah's heart skipped a beat. "Is it Tom? Is Tom there?" Could he have made his way there? How? And yet—

"No, Sarah, not Tom." Michael sounded disappointed. "It's Mr. Johnson, the captain of the wagon train we started out with. They must have gotten here well ahead of us."

"We never did catch up, because of one thing or another," Mrs. Kerber added tersely, looking hard in Sarah's direction.

"Maw, look! Now I recognize some of the others—there's Mrs. Philip—her two boys—the doctor—forget his name."

"Dr. McLean," said Mrs. Kerber. "Didn't do much for your paw, though."

"Looks like we're going to miss the wharf," Michael suddenly shouted. He rushed back to where Sarah was trying desperately to keep her balance and working the board at the same time. "Here, I'll take it. No, we'll both do it. Waggle it more to the right, head for that landing place this side of the wharf!"

There was a loud splash. "Mamie! Mamie!" screamed Sophie, jumping up and down in the rapidly flooding chest. "Man fall in water—"

Someone had jumped off the wharf into the river and was swimming toward them against the current.

"Looks like he's going to try to help steer us toward the landing place," said Sarah's father. "Must be a strong swimmer—or an idiot!"

The man was only a yard from the raft when he disappeared. Sarah's heart skipped a beat. Lost in the surging water, trying to help them . . . Will- hata-nam . . . Will-hata-nam . . .

There was a loud splash as the man's head popped up alongside the raft, and, he grabbed one of the lashed-on wheel spokes. He sputtered and spit out water, started to say something, ducked under again as the current, now sweeping at least a foot over the sinking raft threatened to pull him away.

"Help him, Michael!" Sarah shouted. "I can manage the rudder. Give him something to hang onto."

"Don't need it," the man shouted, popping up again. "I've got hold of this here piece of rope. Now I'll just swim alongside, help you get this darn thing over to the landin' place. Wouldn't trust that Sarah Pearl if I was you! Michael, neither!"

Spitting out a few more mouthfuls of river water, he shook the dark, curly hair out of eyes.

"Why that's—why that's—" stammered Sarah.

"Tom! My Tom!" Sophie started laughing, holding out her arms.

"Your Tom? Your Tom?" Sarah's father sounded incredulous. "This person is Tom Kerber?"

"Tom! Oh, oh," cried Mrs. Kerber. She knelt down in the water sweeping over the edge of the raft and reached out her hand toward him. "My ss-son—my ss-son—"

"Careful, Maw," said Tom. "You're about to fall in. Just hang on, we're almost to shore. Few more shoves—you workin' that rudder back there, Sarah? See, knew I could do it!"

"Tom Kerber? How can that be?" Sarah's father asked again. "You're sure?"

"Of course, Papa. Can hardly believe it myself. We thought he was lost, lost looking for me. He's been missing for almost—almost—" She couldn't remember how long. Her mind was so overwhelmed, so confused.

"And what's old Boone doing on this here raft thing? Looks real out of place, if you ask me." Tom was laughing as he swam alongside, alternatively swimming and shoving.

Mrs. Kerber still knelt on the side of the raft, but because of the shock at seeing Tom, seemed incapable of helping Michael propel the raft by paddling.

"Never you mind, Maw," Michael said, "I'll do it. You just stay put and don't fall off. Best stand up and hang onto the chest."

A few minutes more and the rapidly sinking raft came within several yards of the landing place. Four or five men waded quickly into the water, seized the raft by anything they could hold onto and drew it up onto the grassy bank. Boone, probably pretty nervous with the river movements under him, leaped off first and shook himself hard as if glad to be on land. That lightened the raft so the men could beach it. Michael helped Sarah step down, then lifted Sophie out of the half-water-filled chest, jumped off the raft, and placed her in Sarah's arms.

"Breakfast. Bacon. Breakfast!" she kept repeating.

"Keep ahold her, will you," he said, "while I help Maw off, your father, too."

But Tom had already climbed aboard the raft and was attempting to assist his mother off and onto the grass, despite the fact she kept trying to hug him, push his hair out of his eyes, stroke his face. "My boy, my Tom—"

"Oh stop your fussin', Maw," Tom protested. "Here, don't forget your cane. Good thing it didn't float away. Let's get you off this darn thing. Then I reckon I've got some tellin' to do."

"You sure have, Tom." Michael was pouring water out of his boots. "Best wait a bit, 'til we all get dried off."

I'll take care of that horse for you," a man offered, latching onto his lead rope.

"Let me know where you're goin'," said Tom. "I sure want to go see him later."

"I'll stable him with Mr. Johnson's team for the time being. That lean-to behind the big cabin. He'll be fine. Looks none too happy 'bout almost drowning. Whites of his eyes showing. He's been through a lot, I can tell."

How true, thought Sarah, carrying Sophie up toward the group of cabins. She'd tell Tom all about it, at least her part of Boone's story. Tom, she knew, would have his share to tell.

"If that don't beat all," her father kept muttering. "Who would have thought it."

"Of course that poor horse has been through a lot, Papa. You'd scarcely believe the coincidences."

He looked at her strangely. "No," he said slowly, "no, I didn't mean the horse."

Just then a tall man with a reddish beard, wearing a beaver hat and a black vest over his collarless white shirt, approached them. "Welcome, folks, welcome to Discovery Settlement. After our long wait—a miracle must have brought you here. Yes, from the looks of things, a miracle." He took Mrs. Kerber's hand. "Well, ma'am, how good it is to see your family again. What a pity Mr. Kerber isn't with you, may the Lord rest his soul. But he's with us here in spirit, of that I'm sure."

Mrs. Kerber seemed unable to speak and leaned heavily on her cane, gasping. *It's been too much for her*, Sarah thought, surprised at her own feeling of compassion for the woman.

"And this young man is Michael, is he not?"

"We're thankful to be here at last, sir," Michael said, shaking his hand.

"And this young lady?"

"Sarah Lundgren, and her father, William Lundgren," Michael answered. "Maw says they're distant relations, her side of the family. They're from Four Corners—we stopped off there, hoping to catch up to the wagon train within a few days."

"Pity you didn't." He couldn't seem to take his eyes off Sarah. "Sarah, you said? I thought she was a—Sarah you said? Ahem . . ." He cleared his throat and looked embarrassed. "Well now, my good wife here—you remember Martha? She'll take you and your sons to our cabin. Plenty of room. I believe Mrs. Berzinsky has offered to look after these other folks."

It wasn't long before Sarah and her father were led off up a sloping lane toward a small log cabin just under a stand of aspen trees. Mrs. Kerber, Tom, and Michael were ushered by Mrs. Johnson in the opposite direction toward a larger building, closer to the wharf. Michael carried Sophie on his back, and Tom, with his arm around his mother, half supported her as she haltingly tapped her way with her cane along the stoney path.

"Poor Eliza," commented Sarah's father.

"Sometimes, Papa, events come too quick to understand or even take in."

"There's wisdom in that," he said, pausing to catch his breath as Mrs. Berzinsky guided them up the sloping path.

"I know, Papa," Sarah continued. "It happened to me. Not only once but several times. Some day I'll tell you about it, once you're rested." She stopped to look back. "Oh—but I've got to ask Michael something, Papa. You go on ahead with this kind lady."

"Michael—wait!" she called after him. "I need to speak to you. Will I see you—"

"Of course, you'll see him later," said the woman beside her as she took her arm. "Come along now. Let's get you out of those wet clothes." Mrs. Berzinsky was a short, motherly sort of woman, broad-shouldered, barefoot, wearing a dark blue dress and matching sunbonnet, only loosely tied under her chin. Her whole appearance was comforting, just the sort of woman Sarah longed to see after all those trying months with Mrs. Kerber. She reminded her, in fact, of her own mother and wondered whether her father thought the same.

"Now come along with me," Mrs. Berzinsky said impatiently. "Don't tire your Pa anymore. He looks all in. I'm sure you need a wash up, a change of clothes—both of you. You are a girl, aren't you? Thought so. Might have something in the chest will do. Your Pa, too. Mr. Berzinsky's things might fit him.

Later this evening we're having a celebration, down to Johnsons's cabin. We'll be so glad to celebrate you new comers' arrival. First we've had. Been expecting them Kerbers for some time, you'll need to tell me 'bout you folks. Thank the Lord you got here all right. A lot of trouble on the trail?"

"Some. Yes, some," Sarah slowly answered, with a faint, half smile.

"There were some moments," William Lundgren added, putting his arm around Sarah's shoulders. "Some very strange and wondrous moments, right, my dear? And no doubt more to come."

Sarah was not quite sure what her father meant. But feeling his closeness and knowing he was safe beside her was wondrous enough.

The night and the celebration grew longer as people came and went in and out of the large Johnson cabin beside the landing place. A roaring fire in the large fireplace took the dampness out of the air, air now filled with the smell of coffee, bacon, beef stew, apple cider, and biscuits smothered in gravy. Sarah sat together with Michael on a small bench for two at one side of the fireplace, while on the other side Tom held Sophie, contentedly asleep against his shoulder and clutching a rag doll.

How good to get out of Tom's old clothes, Sarah thought, feeling against her knee the smooth-textured petticoat Mrs. Berzinsky had brought out of a chest along with a number of other things, including an old rag doll which had belonged, she explained, to her now grown daughter. At Sarah's suggestion she happily presented the doll to Sarah for Sophie, who promptly named it Becky and refused to let it out of her sight.

Sitting there beside Michael, feeling the warmth of the fireplace, breathing in the wholesome scents of stew, apples smothered in brown sugar and cinnamon, yeasty bread baking, and coffee, Sarah fingered the gathered folds of the cotton dress Mrs. Berzinsky had laid out for her. It was patterned with pink rosebuds. There was lace edging around the collar, and the long sleeves had a lace frill falling around her wrists. Mrs. Berzinsky also did something with her hair, pinning it up with a tortoise-shell comb in such a way that it looked longer. I'm afraid it'll take a long time to grow out," Mrs. Berzinsky had remarked, teasing the short, stubby ends this way and that until they looked almost respectable.

Sarah was glad she'd refused the corset-underthing with the stays. After the freedom of boys' clothes, as much as she disliked them, that corset would have been unbearable.

She caught Michael staring at her now and then. Didn't he recognize her, transformed back to a girl?

"You've come a long way, Lundgren," remarked Mr. Johnson to Sarah's father, who was stretched out on a cot along the wall, dressed in a pair of Mr. Berzinsky's overalls and a checked wool shirt. One of the women had draped a shawl around his shoulders, claiming he looked peaked and didn't want him to get chilled. Dr. McLean had given him some medicine, which eased his breathing. "And I can tell you, the truth is that your chances of making it alone all the way from Minnesota were one in a million."

"I recognize that, sir. I would never have survived except for a these folks here." He gestured toward the Kerbers. "First, a total stranger found me ailing along the trail, unable to continue. He brought me into a sheltered place, a cave it was, then left on my horse to get help. Fron here. But several days past and he never returned. I was convinced that was the end."

"You've no idea who he was?"

"No, not then. A little later the Kerbers came along in their wagon and I continued the journey with them."

"So here you are," Johnson laughed. "But from the looks of it, that wagon arrived ingeniously re-made into something else, right? A water-going wagon." There was general laughter around the room. "I expect that'll be a story to tell."

"Perhaps we could save that 'til later," said William Lundgren. "Right now, I've a better one. That young man who found me on the trail—I had no idea who he was. He never told me."

"Ah," exclaimed Johnson, "I know—"

Sarah's father raised his hand to interrupt him. "If he had, I would have recognized the name and made some connections. Our families were related several generations back in Ohio. We'd corresponded, planned to meet once your wagon train came through Four Corners. I even had some ideas about persuading them to settle there, near us in Minnesota. Unfortunately, several events intervened. "

Tom was looking very uncomfortable and occupied himself with sliding the now restless Sophie off his lap and onto the floor. "Go on, Sophie, go to Maw," he whispered and gave her a shove in that direction.

"Certainly," Lundgren continued, if that young man had told me his name, I would have recognized it. Perhaps not the Tom, but most certainly the Kerber."

There was a distinct gasp from Mrs. Kerber, a whoop from Michael. "Didn't know who you were neither, sir," said Tom. "Didn't think to ask, neither."

"That was one thing. The other unbelievable thing was the fact that my daughter, with Michael and Eliza Kerber, would bring their wagon to shelter in that very cave. Truly unbelievable! Can one believe in fate, do you think?"

"Fate or not, sir," said Tom, "that time in the cave seems such a long time ago. But you know, back then I was still only a young kid."

It wasn't clear to Sarah whether he was joking or serious. Probably quite serious, she thought, knowing Tom, the self-confident and pesky boy who once claimed he knew ox-talk and everything else. Yet now he seemed much less of a boy, more— she didn't know how to describe it.

"I'm sorry I couldn't get back to you after I left you there, Mr. Lundgren," Tom said. "Tried my best, but then the wagon train came along, and I had to keep on going west with them. Mr. Johnson will tell you all his reasons. As for your horse, sir, he's fine, got me back here all right. Prob'ly already making friends with old Boone and them other horses out in the lean-to. Which reminds me, I'm about to go out renew my acquaintance with him, 'fore it gets much later."

"I'd like to give you that horse, Tom. He's yours. It's the least I can do."

"Thank you, sir. Mighty generous. Hope Boone won't be jealous."

"But now, Tom," broke in Mr. Johnson. "Tell them how you happened to find Lundgren in the first place."

Eagerly, Sarah listened to Tom's story, wondering if it might be connected with her own at the Shakota village. The fact that Boone was in their corral surely was some evidence of that.

"Wasn't sure I'd ever make it," he began, looking rather embarrassed. "Long story. I'll make it short. Not much of a man for words. Went out to look for Miss, here, bring her back to the wagon. Thought she might have fallen out again." He made a face at Sarah. "Then a couple of Indians jumped me, forced me off Boone. Decided they wanted both me and the horse. No idea why. Took me to a big village. I was there for a couple of days. Then a big hulla-ba-loo—noise, arrows everywhere. Next thing I knew I was riding behind one of them on a pony. No idea why, or to where." He paused and rubbed his face, as if recalling something he wanted to forget.

"What happened next? You must have gotten away somehow." Sarah's thoughts took her back to another escape. More than one.

"Sure did," he said with a grin. "Great big storm came up, rain so heavy couldn't see nothing. Lightning hit a tree, came down on us. Next thing I knew I was off that pony, rolling down a hill, ended up in a pool of water. I hung onto some reeds for a while, then crawled out. By that time the rain'd let up. Couldn't hear nothing. So started walking. Morning came, knew to head west. Stumbled onto a wagon trail. Figured you'd already passed that way, so I kept walking. Then later what do I hear but a horse coming along. I hid in the bushes until I could see what it was. Wasn't a wagon, though. Only this man—"

"You can imagine how surprised I was to see this boy spring out of the bushes," William Lundgren called over from his cot.

"Sure was. Me, too. Knew he was ailing so, as soon's I got him into some kind of shelter—big cave it was, I took off on his horse to find help."

"Tom," said Michael, "that was taking a huge risk. Your chances of finding help, even getting back to Sarah's father were—"

"You're quite right. But let me take over Tom's story from here," said Mr. Johnson. "Wasn't long before my wagon train met Tom riding west along the trail on Mr. Lundgren's horse. Fortunately the boy picked the right trail and kept to it. At that point, I faced a big dilemma. Should I turn back to rescue the man Tom mentioned? I might risk the lives of some fifty people, all the families I was bound to get safely to Discovery. Since I calculated we were so close to the Missouri River crossing, the other leaders and I voted to continue. As soon as we got there, we'd send back for the man Tom had met. Along with several armed men, we'd include Dr. McLean as one of our party."

He looked more serious, more thoughtful for a moment while fingering the buttons on his vest. "Of course, our chances then of finding this man still alive, and still undiscovered by any Shakota using that cave for spiritual rites—McLean, who knows about such things, told me that's what they used it for."

"No, sir," interrupted William Lundgren. "You did the right thing. You made the right choice." He waved a hand around the room. "That we're all here together, safe and sound, is proof that it all turned out better than anyone could ever have hoped. That many right choices were made." He looked pointedly at Sarah. "And now, if you don't mind," he added with a wink, "I think I'd like another glass of that excellent Ohio cider to celebrate."

"Me, too," said Tom.

"Me, me want, too," echoed Sophie, still clutching Becky.

"I'm only surprised you have any left, after how many months on the trail?"

"Over six months. But we kept it under lock a key," Johnson grinned, "saving it for just such a wondrous celebration as this."

There was a ripple of laughter throughout the cabin, the rising buzz of happy conversation, the obvious release of tension and anxiety, second helpings passed around. Sophie, now wandering around the room with a mug of cocoa instead of the cider, started yawning.

"Come on Sophie," said Tom, "let's you and me go out for a quick hello to old Boone, 'fore he beds down for the night. We'll be right back."

"Not too long, now, ss-son," Mrs. Kerber warned. "Way past the child's-ss bedtime as-ss it is-ss."

It fact, it wasn't but a few minutes before Tom re-entered the room, carrying Sophie. "Becky wants bed, she says. Only a quick kiss on Boone's muzzle, then she wanted to come back. We stopped, though, to admire that big stallion, the one with the white blaize. I don't recall seeing him before."

"Arrived early yesterday, I believe," Johnson answered. "His owner was in bad shape from dehydration and a festering arm wound of some sort. Dr. McLean's taking care of him, hopes he won't have to amputate. Seems the man's been wandering around the territory for some time, a week or so at least. Fortunately he got picked up by a patrol from Ft. Rice, and they left him here on their way north.

Sarah sprang to her feet. "His name—what's his name?"

"Not sure. He's still resting up at the Haverford's cabin. John, James, Jake—something like that. Looked like a hunter of some sort." He looked puzzled. "Why do you ask?"

"I might—I might—" Sarah couldn't explain. Not just yet. Jake! Jake and Blaize. He'd made it, somehow. Another miracle. She'd go up to see him first thing in the morning. She'd find out what happened to the others, how he happened to find Blaize or Blaize find him. It didn't matter.

Sophie let out a loud wail. "Come, child," said Mrs. Johnson, "you're more than ready for bed. What a long day for you. And you, too, Eliza. I've a cozy warm bed waiting for you in the back room—for both of you. Michael can sleep in the shed with Tom, where he's been making himself at home."

"We'll stay a bit longer here, if you don't mind," Tom ventured. "Haven't had my fill of that stew yet. Most likely my brother neither. How 'bout it Michael?"

"Later, you go ahead. I've some things to discuss with Sarah first."

At this Tom gave a disdainful snort and made his way over to the table, still loaded with food, and proceeded to shovel onto a big tin plate stew, biscuits, apple betty, cornbread, and completing it with three ladles of rich gravy. Holding the full plate on his lap, he sat on the edge of William Lundgren's cot. "We've a few things to talk about, man to man," he explained in between mouthfuls of food." I expect Mr. Lundgren would like to do the same, but maybe a few more sips of Ohio cider might help?"

"Sarah," Michael leaned over to whisper in her ear as they remained by the fireplace, "words don't come easy to me."

"I know that," she whispered back.

"What your father said—about the right thing."

"I'm not sure what he meant."

"I think I know. In fact, I'm sure I know." He paused as if searching for words. "I'm glad you did the right thing. You made the right choice."

Sarah looked surprised. "The right choice? What was that?"

"If you don't know it now, you will soon enough," he blurted out, as he seized her hand and pressed it to his heart. She could feel the beating of it, and it stirred her own emotions. "Our future here ," he continued. "The choice of our future here in Discovery—as future kinfolk. And not distant kinfolk, either!"